Katie Goes to College

On Orthopaedics Sister Beckwith greeted Katie
with a smile. "A student!" she announced. "Well,
we're fully staffed for the first time in a month!"
And everyone looked pleased to see Katie, even
though she was only a mere student.

She remembered her dad's words – "with all them
staff cuts and all…" It looked as if she was in for a
baptism of fire! Obviously everyone expected her to
get stuck in.

Beaming back at Sister Beckwith, Katie asked,
"Right – where do I start?"

In the same series:

Claire's Conquests

Look out for:

Jan's Journey

Point

NURSES

Katie Goes to College

Bette Paul

■SCHOLASTIC

Scholastic Children's Books
7–9 Pratt Street, London NW1 0AE, UK
a division of Scholastic Publications Ltd
London ~ New York ~ Toronto ~ Sydney ~ Auckland

First published by Scholastic Publications Ltd, 1995

ISBN 0 590 13181 8

Typeset by TW Typesetting, Midsomer Norton, Avon

Printed by Cox & Wyman Ltd, Reading, Berks.

Chapter 1

"'Bye! 'Bye, Gary – see you soon!" Katie Harding leaned out of the window and waved to the fast-disappearing figure on the platform. As soon as he was out of sight she pushed the window up, leaned against it and breathed a sigh of relief. Thank goodness that was over!

Leaving Gary at home was like leaving part of herself; they'd known each other all their lives, through school and into college – "Gary-and-Katie": always a couple. Almost a habit. And yet… Katie had to admit that she was glad to leave Gary to his A-levels and get away all on her own. After all, it was what she'd been working at for years – the start of her nursing career.

Katie grinned to herself. Look out, St Agatha's Hospital – here I come! Or should she call it

Brassington General, now, she wondered. Well, she'd soon find out. And, delving into one of the many pockets in her rugged anorak, she produced a medical text book. Might as well start as she meant to go on.

"Brassington Central! Passengers are reminded to take all their luggage with them. This train terminates here. All change!"

The train glided into the station and Katie stepped down on to the platform. She was in the last compartment and faced a long walk up the platform. Ah well, a nurse had to be fit, and she was that all right! Hauling a loaded rucksack, almost as tall as herself, up on to her shoulders, she strode out past First Class, head held high.

So high that she failed to notice a well-dressed girl standing by a pile of luggage.

"Oops – sorry!" said Katie, as she swerved to avoid an expensive-looking suitcase.

"Oh – so sorry – it's in the way – terribly sorry…"

The girl's voice was soft and light, the accent upper-class. Katie quickly noted the loose cream coat, the silk scarf, the shining, ash-blonde hair and the expensive perfume.

"That's all right, love!" She grinned cheerily up at the girl and strode off as firmly as if she was out for the day on her beloved fells.

*   *   *

But the walk to the hospital was nothing like fell-walking. On the crowded streets the top-heavy rucksack got in everyone's way and her hiking boots were too heavy for walking on hard pavements. With aching shoulders and throbbing feet, Katie eventually arrived at the entrance to Brassington General Hospital feeling as if she'd run the Three Peaks Race. Well, she consoled herself, soon she'd be in her own little bedsit at the nurses' hostel.

Not yet awhile. The porter pointed across the grounds towards a copse of birch trees. "Kelham House? Over there, love, through the trees. Shall you manage?"

She nodded. Of course she'd manage. She always did. But the straps of her rucksack dug deep and she felt every ridge of her mountain boots as she plodded what felt like the last ten miles home.

"Ms Kate Harding … mmm … now, let's see where we've put you…" Katie had a moment of panic as she watched the smartly-suited woman run a red fingernail up and down a list. What if her room hadn't been reserved? She was sure she'd filled in the right form – Dad had insisted. She swallowed hard and eased her rucksack off her shoulder.

"Ah – yes – here we are!" The shiny red lips parted in half a smile. "New student – third floor – Room 9. Right?" Katie nodded and bent to pick up the rucksack.

"You'll need these." She offered Katie a key and what looked like a credit card. "The card's for the outside door and this is the key to your room. Right?"

Katie mumbled her thanks, picked up the rucksack and turned to look for a lift.

"Up the stairs, left at the top," said the woman, brightly. "Right?"

"Right," said Katie, grimly, slinging an arm into the strap of the dreaded rucksack and stumping off up the first flight of stairs. Why oh why hadn't she listened to Dad when he'd advised her to take the suitcase? Well, she had insisted she'd need her rucksack for weekend hikes. Brassington General was close to the Peak District, after all.

"You'll be too whacked," her dad had warned. "What with all them staff cuts and all."

Well, she had to admit he was right: she was too whacked – already! As she plodded up the third flight she promised herself that very, very soon she'd dump the over-loaded rucksack with her over-heated anorak, pull off her over-heavy boots, and sink down on her own little bed in her own little room.

On the top landing she hesitated. "Left," she muttered to herself. "Right?"

"Pardon?" A dark, anxious-looking lad was peering at her.

"Oh … er … Room 9," she said.

"Is down…" He indicated the corridor and held up three fingers. "Tree on ze left." His foreign accent was even stronger than her Yorkshire one, she noticed.

"Right." She nodded and went on.

"No, left," he called after her.

Left, right, left, right, they seemed to be the only words she'd heard lately! And the lad was right – number 9 was the third on the left. Giggling feebly at her joke and shaking with exhaustion, Katie unlocked the door – her door – and let herself into her room. Home – at last!

WELCOME TO KELHAM!
Sister Ann Thomas invites you to take tea
– and ask questions –
at 15.00 this afternoon in the Common Room.

The printed card lay on top of a glossy folder on the desk/dressing-table by the window. Katie, refreshed and rested now, and dressed in her usual blue jeans and sweatshirt, glanced around the room. What a mess! She'd emptied the rucksack and was in the process of stowing all her stuff away in the cupboards and wardrobes which fitted along one wall of the little room. Such luxury! thought Katie, accustomed to the rickety old bits and pieces which made up her bedroom at home. With fittings like this, even she could be tidy – given time!

She moved over to the washbasin and peered at the cabinet and shelves above it. Goodness – there was enough space for a chemist's shop! She emptied her small toilet bag into the basin and began to stack the shelves with soap, toothpaste, toothbrush, deodorant, talc... There was still a lot of space left. She made a mental note to buy a few medicaments to fill some of it up.

Picking up her new travelling alarm clock, her Christmas present from Gary, she gasped. It was ten past three already and the invitation from Sister Thomas was obviously an order! Grabbing her folder and key, she rushed out of the door, slammed it behind her, jumped downstairs two at a time and fell into a heap of bags and cases.

"Upsadaisy!" She felt herself lifted from the pile of luggage and stood to face a strong, stocky man, with a mop of fair hair and the kind of suntan she'd always dreamed of acquiring.

"You all right?" he enquired, stacking the pieces of luggage which she'd disturbed.

"Yes thanks... Er ... sorry..." Katie blushed and turned to help him but he was too quick for her. Too strong as well, she noticed, as he picked up three suitcases at once. Dazed, Katie stared at them and wondered why they looked familiar.

"Are you ready, you two?" A light, slightly-Welsh voice interrupted Katie's thoughts. "Leave your luggage against the wall now and come in to tea."

The uniformed nurse, obviously used to being obeyed, led the way into the next room.

The blond man straightened up. "After you," he said, coolly, indicating the doorway.

Blushing, and hating herself for it, Katie walked past him and entered a tall, light room, decorated in muted golden colours with glossy white paint. She stood for a second, relishing the space, the trees framing the huge sash windows. And the laden tea-table.

"Always hungry, nurses," Sister Thomas was explaining. "Though this is the only time we actually serve tea. After today, you get your own – there's a kitchen on each floor." She smiled all round the room at the students. She was nice, thought Katie, relaxing enough to help herself to a cup of tea, three sandwiches and a very large piece of fruit cake. The blond chap took only a cup of tea, then went and sat on the window-seat alone, making it quite clear he didn't want company. Katie looked for a place across the room.

The thin, very dark foreign boy she'd met on the stairs was sitting in the middle of a sofa; the plate on the low table in front of him was piled high with sandwiches. Well, at least somebody was hungrier than she was, thought Katie.

"Could I sit here?" she smiled.

For a moment he looked blankly at her, then he nodded, nervously, several times. Oh, well done,

Katie Harding! she thought. One bloke thinks you're a clumsy idiot, another is obviously terrified of you. So much for Dad's idea of making friends and influencing people!

"Maybe I'll join you?" said a voice from the boy's other side.

Katie looked up and saw a tall girl with a mass of black hair cascading round her clear white face.

"Yes – come and sit down," Katie invited, relieved to share the dark boy's awkwardness.

The girl smiled, shyly. "Thanks," she murmured. She sat down and drank her tea eagerly, as if she'd waited all day for it.

"Right – all feeling a bit refreshed?" Sister Thomas pulled out a chair and sat at the head of the group. "There's a lot to learn these first few days, so we'd better start right away."

She explained that she was their own personal tutor, and went on to tell them something of the arrangements at Kelham House.

"Now, if you'll just refer to your folder..." she said.

And for the next half-hour she took them through maps of the hospital, lists of names, time-tables, room plans, schedules, until Katie's head was quite whirling.

"Don't worry, you'll be able to work it all out later." Sister Thomas stood in the centre of the room and looked slowly round at the six new students. "You must understand that Kelham students are special to me," she said. "I pick and choose my students, and I like to think I get the best of them." She paused and looked hard at each student in turn. "I chose each one of you because I felt you had something special to bring to nursing, something more than high exam results and a good school record. And it's that special something that will be needed in this, our centenary year. More about that – and the Centenary Committee – once you've got settled in. We have a tutorial booked in two weeks' time. I'll meet you all here again – though I can't promise a tea like this one! Any questions?"

Katie felt that she had at least twenty of them, but she couldn't decide where to start.

"Yes. What about uniform?" The man in the window-seat spoke up.

"Ah, yes – well, that's just for your ward days, which you six will start tomorrow. Other days you're students, free to dress like any students in any college anywhere. All right?" Sister Thomas paused but no one spoke. "Now, tomorrow morning is the inaugural lecture – I'll see you all then. Meantime, I suggest you introduce yourselves."

Sister Thomas beamed all round, and left them to finish their tea.

Katie looked around the room. Alone in the window-seat, the blond man was reading his folder. On a low chair nearby, a stunningly beautiful black girl stretched out her long, smooth legs, lifted her arms and yawned, languorously, or was it insolently? Katie couldn't decide which. She turned her attention to the remaining student, seated on an upright chair near the door. Katie frowned; with her fine black sweater, full creamy skirt and patent moccasins, there was something about her... Her thoughts were interrupted by the man at the window.

"Well, I want to get back up to sort out my room so I suggest we get on..."

He sounded older, more in command of himself than the average student, thought Katie, with interest. Good looking, too!

"I'm Nick Bone," the blond man went on. "Redundant merchant-seaman searching for a new career." He turned abruptly to the black girl. "Your turn!" he said.

She flicked a cool glance over him. "Like yourself," she said, in a deep, husky voice, "I'm changing careers. Barbara Robinson's the name." She turned her glance to the three on the sofa.

"Claire Donovan." The tousled-haired girl spoke with a marked Irish accent. "I'm over from Donegal – and will it be all right if I pour some more tea?" she smiled. Relaxed by her warmth, they all held out their cups.

As Claire sat down again, she nudged the boy in the middle.

"My name is Jan Buczowski." He said it dully, as

if under interrogation. "I am a student … *was* a student before the war in my country." He stopped, looked blankly ahead, and took a huge bite out of a sandwich. There was an awkward silence.

Katie was embarrassed by silences. "I'm Katie Harding, from over the tops – that's Yorkshire." She knew she spoke too brightly, too loudly. She blushed and turned towards the girl at the door.

"Nicola Browne – Nikki." Although she'd scarcely spoken, they all heard the clipped, upper-class accent. But Katie was the only one who recognized it. That luggage, that classy girl, that cut-glass voice – it was the First Class passenger on Platform Three, the one she'd almost knocked over! The one whose luggage she'd completely knocked over! Katie groaned inwardly; what on earth would this cool, classy girl think of her? But Nikki Browne looked straight ahead and gave no sign of recognition.

In fact she didn't say anything more. The tea-party broke up with bits of conversation – Barbara Robinson talking to Nick Bone, who was nearest her, and the three on the sofa, rather hampered by Jan's stumbling English, exchanging a few words. Nicola Browne, sitting apart from the rest, gazed serenely round the room, saying nothing.

An hour later, Katie was shifting bundles of clothes from cupboard to drawer and back again. No matter how she arranged them, she had barely enough to fill half the fitted cupboards. Maybe if she took the socks and tights out of the underwear drawer and hung the blouses with the skirts and trousers in the wardrobe? She opened the wardrobe doors and gazed at the few things hanging there: her black jeans, jacket, a couple of skirts, her nearly-new nurse's cloak and her uniform dress.

Struck by a sudden thought, she turned to the folder lying on her bed. Quickly she riffled through the mass of papers and pulled out a blue timetable. Just as she feared: Wednesday was ward day – and that was tomorrow. She looked back at the blue-checked dress in the wardrobe and her stomach churned at the thought of tomorrow. Or was that just hunger? She looked around vaguely, wishing she'd accepted Dad's parting gift of cheese-and-pickle sandwiches. They'd do nicely for supper right now.

The sound of distant voices filtered up the corridor and she wondered if the others were going over to the canteen. If they were, they hadn't invited her to join them.

Katie sighed. "Special students", Sister Thomas had called them. Well, she didn't feel at all special just then, just tired and hungry and rather lonely. The voices on the corridor grew louder now, almost angry, followed by a thump or two and the final slam of a door. Somebody, obviously very angry, stumped off downstairs. More out of a desire for human contact than curiosity, Katie opened her door and peeped out.

There was a pile of luggage stacked outside one of the bedsit doors. THE luggage. Perhaps she could make up for her previous gaffe and help the girl – Nikki, wasn't it? Katie went quickly to the other end of the corridor and found the door open. Inside was Nikki Browne, sitting at the dressing-table, bolt upright and obviously very tense.

"Hi – can I give you a hand with your luggage?" Katie asked.

"Thank you, no," said Nikki Browne, coldly.

Katie flushed and laughed nervously. "I think you should fetch it in before another idiot falls over it," she joked.

Nikki didn't laugh. "No point," she said. "Someone's already moved in – see?"

And, looking round, Katie did indeed see. The room was bigger than hers – and much neater. Books were already stacked on the shelves, the open wardrobe door revealed several hangers with trousers and jackets on them and on the dressing-table, right in front of Nikki, an array of aftershave and very expensive colognes – for men.

"So this is the wrong room?" Katie asked.

"This is the right room; the room I was given." Katie was surprised to hear the tremor in Nikki's voice. Obviously she was not the cool, detached operator she liked to appear.

"But who's moved in?" she asked.

"That *man* – Mr Bone. You remember, he had tea with us."

Katie nodded thoughtfully. "Ah – there must have been a mix-up over your names," she observed. "Nick Bone – Nikki Browne – computer error, as they say."

"That's no consolation," said Nikki, bitterly. "One of us will have to move – and he's determined it shall be me."

"I don't see why," said Katie, ever ready to take up the female cause. "You just stand your ground – I would."

"I'm sure you would." The voice came from behind her. Nick Bone's quiet, laid-back voice. "However, this is not your battle so perhaps you'd leave Miss Browne and myself to settle it."

Flushing with anger, Katie looked across at Nikki, hoping for a bit of support. Nikki merely raised an eyebrow and gave a tight little smile. Well, so much for sisterhood, thought Katie, backing out of the doorway.

Back in her room she suddenly realized she was trembling – with rage? Or was it shame? How to Win Friends and Influence People, she thought bitterly; at this rate I'll be spending the next three years on my own! Blinking back tears, she looked round the room, bare and empty now that her things had been put away. She'd have given anything to be back home just then, in her cramped, messy room, with the scent of cooking seeping upstairs, and Dad calling her down to tea…

"Katie… Katie?" There was a knock on her door. "Katie, it's me – Claire Donovan – you know?"

Katie leaped up, grabbed a tissue and blew her nose loudly before opening the door.

"Hi!" she said, over-cheerfully. "What can I do for you?"

"I was wondering were you hungry?" Claire said in her soft Irish voice. "I have enough food for half the hospital in my box – Barbara and Jan are already cooking something up in the kitchen. Will you not join us?"

Would she not! Katie ran her hands through her short, straight hair and brushed them down her sweatshirt.

"Come as you are," smiled Claire. "We're none of us smart. But don't forget to lock your room."

Katie looked round the neat, bare room. White walls, white fittings, brown carpet and bed-cover. Well, perhaps it would feel like home one day! She closed the door, locked it and sniffed, hungrily now. Was that the scent of new bread? She followed it along the corridor to the kitchen – and her first meal at Kelham House.

Chapter 2

"Hey, look at that!" Katie pointed to the team of painters on the scaffolding high above the entrance to St Ag's. They were working on the Gothic lettering of a huge old sign – "St Agatha's Royal Infirmary". Underneath the original date, a carpenter was fixing a new one – a hundred years later. "Sister Thomas said we were special, but I didn't think we were all *that* special!" she laughed.

"It's not for us," Claire said. "It's for the centenary. Come on in here!" She led the way into the vast entrance hall, where the smell of paint was stronger even than the usual hospital smell. "They'll be doing the place up, I'm thinking."

"Ready for the sale?" asked Katie.

"What?"

"Well, it seems to me that they do places up to sell them off – you know, the mines, the factories – the hospitals…"

Claire looked shocked. "They can't sell hospitals, surely?" she said.

Katie smiled, grimly. "Sell anything, some folks," she said. "Especially if it's going well." She shook her slightly shabby cloak off her shoulders and followed her friend through the glass doors into the main corridor.

"Let's find breakfast!" she suggested.

The staff canteen was closed – for decorating – and a notice told them that staff could use the visitors' café on block E.

"But that's miles away," protested Katie, remembering the map in her folder. "By the time we've been over there and got something to eat, we'll be late back to the teaching block."

Claire nodded. "I think we'll be getting over to the inaugural lecture," she agreed. "Let's hope there's a coffee machine."

"Well, anyway, I'm too nervous to eat," Katie confessed. "And we did have that lovely meal last night." Claire had fed them with fresh soda-bread, potato scones with rashers and quantities of sweet, strong tea. And what she called "good crack" to follow. Which meant that they chatted happily together, helping Jan out with his English whenever necessary. By the time she'd snuggled into her new, strange bed, Katie had forgotten her bout of home-sickness.

"It was a great evening," she said now, "and thanks for the food."

"My folks will always be sending parcels," smiled Claire. "They seem to think I'll be starving over here."

"They may well be right," Katie laughed, "if our first breakfast is anything to go by."

But Claire's hope was fulfilled – not only a coffee machine, but crisps and chocolate too. Katie winced as she fed the coins into the slot. She'd have to make sure she had enough time to get to the café for cheap meals in future – and enough money! Katie was well aware that her student grant was not going to see her through the year and Dad had little enough to spare.

In the lecture room, Katie looked around for the rest of the Kelham students. She saw that Jan and Nick Bone were sitting together. Jan looked up and smiled across at her, but Nick Bone sat, grim-faced, without even the flicker of a glance. He didn't look at all happy.

Katie suddenly remembered the embarrassing confrontation the previous evening. She turned to ask Claire if she'd heard anything but before she could speak, Sister Thomas and some other people came on to the platform at the front of the room. Silence fell as one of the men stepped forward.

He was a huge man, not only tall, but broad and

fleshy. He had a large head with a mass of long white hair brushed back from a craggy old face which had once been handsome. Still was, Katie thought, but formidable – oh, yes. She shivered. Not the sort of man you'd want to be on the wrong side of.

His bright blue eyes glinted like steel but his voice was warm and ever-so-slightly Welsh. "Good morning to you all. I'm Mr Lester-Ellis – Orthopaedics is my department. I look forward to meeting you on my wards over the coming months. Meanwhile I'm here to welcome you to the College of Nursing and especially to this hospital." He paused and gazed round the whole room, eyes gleaming sharply from beneath his wild eyebrows. "Whether you call this place Brassington General Hospital, St Agatha's Royal Infirmary or even St Ag's…" He smiled broadly and Katie felt like giving an answering grin – but she didn't dare.

Mr Lester-Ellis frowned and his voice took on a serious note. "Whatever it's called, and whatever its future, this is one of the oldest teaching hospitals in the north – a hundred years old this very year it is. You are all very lucky to be here in such an historic place at such an historic time." He paused and gazed round again, as if challenging the students to believe him. "Of course, we are lucky to be able to choose from among the best students in the country – that's you!" Another pause, another keen look round at the students, who were relaxing now, basking in this flattering assessment of themselves.

The smug smiles soon faded when Mr Lester-Ellis spoke again. "So now it's up to you to prove us right, isn't it?" He paused and seemed to fix the whole assembly with his hawk-like stare. Then, just as the silence was becoming unbearable, he turned and swept off the platform.

Katie was almost ready to applaud. What an exit! she thought. Perfect timing! The students sat in silence, still stunned by the performance. Katie went on looking at the place where Mr Lester-Ellis had been standing; she shivered.

"Imagine facing him in the ward!" she whispered to Claire.

But Claire smiled. "Ach, it's just the Celt in him. He's probably just a pussy-cat really."

"Like a tiger, you mean?" Katie was not convinced. But before she could argue further the College Principal stepped forward.

"Welcome to St Ag – er, Brassington General." Mrs Grayson smiled at her own indecision. "Well, sometime soon we may even know our official name. You've arrived here at a time of change: in the way we train nurses, the way we run hospitals – even the way we finance them. You may think that none of this is going to affect you, but believe me, it will. All I can tell you just now is to try to keep up with new developments as well as with your work. So I'll hand you over to your personal tutors now." She turned and indicated that the rest of the staff should leave the platform.

Katie was surprised to discover that Sister Thomas's group consisted of about a dozen day-students as well as the Kelham six. Some of them looked nearly as old as Dad, she thought, eyeing the tough, stocky man who stood next to her. And suddenly, there it was again, a pang of homesickness. How on earth was Dad managing, all on his own?

But the thought was only brief; Sister Thomas was speaking.

"Kelham students – Wednesday is your ward day this term so I may as well get rid of you first." She moved among the Kelham six handing yellow cards to each one.

"These are your ward slips," she said, as they took them. "You'll need to show them as it's your first day on. Now – let me see – ah, yes, Katie Harding…"

"Thank you, Sister." Katie took the slip and casually glanced down. "Porchester Ward," she read. "Sister Beckwith." She looked up. "What ward is that?" she asked, brightly.

Sister Thomas looked straight at her. "Orthopaedics," she replied. And she smiled.

With mixed feelings, Katie made her way along the highly-polished corridors to Porchester Ward. Part of her was eager to get on the wards; she'd had plenty of lectures the past two years at FE college. But Orthopaedics – Mr Lester-Ellis's own department! That wasn't at all what she wanted; she'd hoped for Accident and Emergency, or even the Children's Ward. Well, all she'd got was broken legs and arms, and hip and knee replacements. Not much chance to show how "special" she was with elderly ladies trying out new hips and Mr Lester-Ellis lording it over everybody!

On Orthopaedics Sister Beckwith greeted her with a smile. "A student!" she announced. "Well, we're fully staffed for the first time in a month!" And everyone looked pleased to see Katie, even though she was only a mere student.

She remembered her dad's words – "with all them staff cuts and all…" It looked as if she was in for a baptism of fire! Obviously everyone expected her to get stuck in.

Beaming back at Sister Beckwith, Katie asked, "Right – where do I start?"

Weeks later Katie remembered that question with a wry grin. It was as though Sister Beckwith had wound her up that morning and her clock had never stopped since! "Observe this, pass me that, would you like to try your hand at…" And then, the very next day into lectures, discussions, seminars and "spare time" in the library, copying up anatomy notes. She couldn't remember a time when she'd been so busy, so tired – and so excited! And not only by the nursing.

Ever since Sister Thomas had mentioned the Centenary Committee, Katie had been determined to join. She loved committees; she'd often helped Dad with his meetings, arranging chairs, handing out tea, sorting papers, photocopying reports – all the jobs her mum used to do with him. At school she'd been a pupil-governor and at college she'd been Chair of the Students' Union. It would be almost like being home, she decided, signing her name with her usual italic flourish. But a lot better – this was real adult stuff.

It was only when she looked up the list and saw Nick Bone's name there that Katie began to have doubts. Why was the superior, solitary Nick Bone volunteering to help with the centenary celebrations? He'd already made it quite clear to the other five that he wanted no part in their social life; at Kelham he never shared a coffee in the kitchen or joined them in the common room. There was something very self-contained about him which irritated Katie, and she wasn't at all sure she wanted to be part of any committee he was on.

But she left her name on the list.

When Katie joined the others in the common room for Sister Thomas's tutorial she felt as if she'd been at St Ag's for six months – and as if she'd aged ten years.

"Hi, everybody. Mind if I sit quietly in the corner and nod off?" she said.

"I don't think you'd get away with it," smiled Claire. "Not with Sister Thomas."

"Not indeed," Jan agreed. "So what is it she wants to talk to us for?"

"Maybe she's gonna tell us who's for the chop," suggested Barbara.

"What do you mean?" asked Nikki anxiously.

"Well, they've been watching our every move, you know, at lectures, in discussions – and especially on the ward!" Barbara's mother was a teaching nurse, so she knew all about it. "Maybe it's assessment time," she said casually, as if it didn't very much matter.

But to Nikki Browne it obviously did. "They can't have made a fair assessment of us by now, surely?" Her usually serene face was creased with anxiety, her blue eyes almost tearful.

She must have had a bad time on Children's, thought Katie, rather smugly; she'd actually enjoyed her ward days – so far.

"They're doing nothing of the kind," soothed Claire. "Calm yourself, Nikki! This is only a tutorial – that's what Sister Thomas called it. She probably holds a session every week or two, just to help sort out any problems."

And Claire was right. Sister Thomas had brought them together to see how they were getting on. But as nobody would admit to having problems she soon went on to talk about the arrangements for St Agatha's Centenary.

"Although we have appointed a co-ordinator for the whole event, most of the celebrations will depend on volunteers," Sister Thomas said. "And I expect my first-year students to get involved – as two of you already have. Well done, Katie and Nick!"

Katie blushed right up to the roots of her sand-coloured curls; it was like being the class swot back at school! Nick Bone, she observed, flashed one of his charming smiles at Sister and ignored everyone else.

Sister Thomas merely nodded at both of them and went on, "There's a tradition at St Ag's that the first-year students perform an entertainment, usually at Christmas. But this year we've brought that forward: there will be a summer show as part of the celebrations." She beamed at them all, collectively now. "And you'll all be in it, I'm sure."

Pause. Silence. Shifty looks. Horror-stricken faces. Then Katie, unable to bear the embarrassing silence as usual, spoke up. "Who's the producer?" she asked.

"You are," smiled Sister Thomas. Katie stared at her. "At least," Sister amended, "one of you is. You're responsible at least for Kelham's part in the entertainment. The other two houses will be planning their part, and the non-residents of course, though it's always more of a problem for them."

More silence. This time Barbara broke it.

"What about money?" she asked.

Sister Thomas nodded. "There's a central committee looking after funds. When you have some idea as to how much you'll need for costume, props, sets and so on, just come to me with a written request – all itemized, of course."

Barbara nodded. "I can do all that," she said. "I was training to be an accountant before ... before I came here."

"Well, there you are," said Sister Thomas. "Each one of you has something special to bring, not only to your nursing but to St Ag's Centenary." She stood up. "Tuesday will be your Kelham Entertainments evening. I've arranged for you to have sole use of this room as from now." She smiled brightly all round. "Well, good luck – I know you won't let me down!"

After she left, there was another awkward silence. Then suddenly everyone spoke at once.

"I came here for a medical training, not to be an actor..." This was Nick Bone, surly as ever.

"Well, actually, I don't think I can do anything entertaining..." Nikki Browne was telling Barbara.

"She was meaning that we will, er ... perform?" Jan turned to Claire for confirmation.

She nodded. "You might be able to do something from your own country," she suggested.

"And you also," he grinned, reminding Claire that she was a foreigner too.

For once Katie wasn't talking. She was thinking hard. Although her chosen career was nursing, her secret passion was acting. She'd acted in all the school plays and several at her FE college. Acted, not starred; nobody ever suggested she was star material. Batty grannies were her speciality, or the ugly best-friend to the heroine. But the previous summer a hard-pressed producer of the college musical had told her that she was a born stage-manager. "I'd never have got it all together without you," she'd said, admittedly after a few glasses of wine at the last-night party. But for a day or two after that, Katie had wondered whether she was on the wrong tack with the pre-nursing diploma course. And now, perhaps she had a chance to find out.

"Well, I don't mind making a start," she said, avoiding Nick Bone's scowl. "You tell me what you can do and I'll try to work out some sort of pro-gramme. We could meet here next week and put it all together – all right?"

"That's the idea, Katie, my girl!" said Claire. "I've done a bit of ceilidh myself – I'm sure I can brush up the odd song."

"And I…" Jan began, then paused to collect his

words. "I play the violin – the folk songs, dances, of my country. But alas! I have not an instrument."

Katie smiled at him. "You will have," she assured him. "Put that on top of your list, Barbara."

And Barbara took out a little red notebook and solemnly entered "1 violin" on a clean page. "That will make a hole in the centenary budget," she grinned.

And another awkward pause. Neither Nick Bone nor Nikki Browne spoke. Nick Bone had turned to look out of the window and Nikki, twitching her hair back and blinking hard, looked even more anxious about the show than she had about the non-existent assessment.

Though perhaps it did exist, Katie suddenly realized. There was more to nursing than lectures, exams and bed-pans. Maybe they'd be judged on their abilities to join in with the community on a project like this.

"Right then!" She spoke more confidently than she felt. "So we'll all think it over and bring some ideas back next Tuesday."

"It's a great idea, Katie," said Claire, eagerly. "And I've just thought – there's a few Irish clubs over here would help…"

Aware of the stony silence from the other two, Katie judged it tactful to leave. She turned at the door and made a mock bow. "A week today, then!"

*   *   *

Up in her room, Katie took out a new flip pad and wrote "Kelham Revue" in black felt-tip on its cover. On the first page she wrote:

Jan – fiddle
Claire – Irish songs
Barbara – finance and ?
Nikki Browne – ?
Nick Bone – ?
Katie Harding – Producer.

She read it through, then pulled a wry face. "Producer" was a bit pompous. What on earth was she going to produce? Wild gypsy violin music and Irish songs hardly added up to thirty minutes' entertainment. What they needed was a dramatic idea… Sighing, she reached up to the bookshelf above her desk. Passing over an ancient copy of Gray's *Anatomy* and half-a-dozen nursing texts, she pulled out a book of one-act plays she'd used at college. Nothing suitable in that, she thought, remembering the problems they'd had with a cast of ten men, three women.

But she was wrong. As she flipped over the pages, something fell out on to the desk top.

"Ah!" Katie almost squealed. "Eureka!"

And she picked up a dark blue folded sheet – the programme of last summer's college play. On the front was the sinister outline of a bowler-hatted, heavily painted young man, leering, winking. "Wilkommen! Bienvenue!! Welcome!!!" The words emerged from his luscious red lips via a speech bubble.

"Cabaret! That's what we'll do," Katie told herself. Not, of course, the full-scale musical they'd done in college. But the idea. Something for everyone, she thought: song, dance, instrumental, jokes, sketches… Everyone could do something like that.

Couldn't they?

Chapter 3

From then on Katie could think of little else but the centenary celebrations. That was easy enough in college; she could make notes about the show as well as the skeleton. But things weren't so simple on her ward day: there was always someone needing her full attention.

Miss Maudie Royston, for instance. Katie was already quite fond of Maudie, a frail old lady of ninety-plus with a pinned hip. She was always lively and good-humoured but had the appetite of a bird – no one could persuade her to finish a meal. And meals were one of Katie's few responsibilities.

"Come on, Miss Royston, just have a taste," Katie cajoled at lunch-time. "It's really good soup, you know." She took the metal cover off the bowl and the aroma of vegetable soup rose into her face. "I could just eat this myself," she said, truthfully.

"What a good idea!" agreed Maudie, in her deep, well-educated voice. "Help yourself, my dear, you need it more than I do."

"Oh, I'm not allowed to," laughed Katie. "It's all for you. Come on, just try a sip."

"And then you'll leave me in peace?"

Katie nodded. "If you promise to eat all your soup."

Maudie Royston took the proffered spoon in a shaky hand and tasted the smallest sip from it. "It's all right," she agreed. "Off you go, now, I can manage it myself."

Feeling rather proud that she'd succeeded where others had often failed, Katie moved on. She went to help an auxiliary nurse push the heavy hot cupboard round the wards and hand out the trays. And when that was done, it was time to start collecting the trays from the other end. Katie paused at Maudie's bedside and peered into the soup-bowl.

"Hey, you've eaten every drop of your soup," she exclaimed, with delight – and pride.

Maudie Royston smiled angelically. "Now perhaps you'd help me up on to my bed," she suggested. "I'm so full up and quite sleepy."

Katie hesitated. Elderly patients were not allowed to stay in bed, unless they were totally immobile, but, after all, Maudie had eaten all her soup and she was nodding off already. It seemed cruel to leave her sitting in her chair.

"Well, just on top of the bed, mind," Katie told her. "And only until they bring afternoon tea." She put her arm across the old lady's back and lifted her up out of the chair and on to her feet.

"Steady… There you go!" Katie guided the old lady across to the bed, and lowered her on to it. She lifted up Maudie's elegantly trousered legs, took off her pretty velvet slippers and plumped up her pillows. "Now, are you comfortable?" she asked.

"Thank you so much, my dear," Maudie murmured, already half asleep.

Katie hovered uneasily by the bed, still unsure that she'd done the right thing, but there was no one around to advise her.

Suddenly Katie heard a rather frantic voice from the men's ward next door and rushed off to clear up the coffee and ice-cream which a heavily plastered arm had just knocked all over the floor.

Then she had to go down to the kitchens to beg another portion for the protesting old man. They were already preparing supper down there and Katie's mouth watered at the smell: Sister Thomas had been right when she said that nurses were always hungry. But there was no time to linger in the hope of a snack – she had to rush back to observe the drugs round!

Well, at least that's more interesting than feeding

time, thought Katie, though she was only allowed to supply the water needed for taking pills. She followed Staff Nurse Howe and Jimmy, the third-year student, as they pushed the drugs trolley, checked charts, and doled out even simple aspirin with solemnity and care. This was always a quiet time on the wards: patients were nicely full of lunch, rather drowsy, and visitors would not arrive for another hour. A gentle word of enquiry – "Need a drink?" – a sympathetic smile, and off to the next bed. One of the few peaceful moments in Katie's frantic ward day.

She smiled at the young woman lying flat on her bed, wincing with pain from her prolapsed disc, and held the beaker of water close to her lips. This really felt like nursing! she thought. Helping someone in pain – and of course she'd persuaded Maudie to eat a whole bowl of soup! For the first time since she'd been at St Ag's, Katie felt a surge of confidence.

It soon dispersed.

"And what's this then, Maudie?" Staff Nurse Howe and Jimmy stood over the recumbent old lady. "How on earth did you get up there?" Staff asked, in a worried tone. "You know you're not allowed to stand without help…"

"Shhh!" Maudie roused herself enough to hold up a warning finger. "Stop that noise, please. You're spoiling my afternoon nap!"

"You'll spoil more than your afternoon nap, my lady, if you keep getting back into bed on your own!" Staff shook her head. "Now, come on, let's have you in the chair!" She nodded to Jimmy and together they grasped Maudie under her shoulders.

"No – no!" Maudie protested. "I ate all my lunch, didn't I?"

"What's that got to do with it?" asked Staff, relaxing her hold for a moment.

"That polite little gel told me I could take a nap on my bed after lunch." Maudie wriggled free of Staff's restraining hand, sat straight up and pointed across the drugs trolley – to Katie!

"Oh, she did, did she?" Staff said, grimly. "Well, Student Nurse Harding isn't running this ward; I am." She looked straight at Katie then turned back to the old lady. "You must sit upright during the day. It's for your own good, you know. Come on, let's have you back in your chair!"

The two nurses lifted the old lady off the bed and settled her into the chair by the window, with a stool to support her legs and a rug to keep them warm.

"There you are, Maudie," Jimmy said, very loudly. "You can have your little nap before your daughter comes to see you." Remembering how particular that daughter was, he leaned back to straighten a pot-plant on the nearby locker.

"Ugh! What's this stuff?" Jimmy looked with dismay at the thick, cold fluid seeping out of the pot over his hands and into his sleeves. "Oh, hell and damnation – somebody's been sick!" he groaned.

But the aroma which rose from his hands was unmistakable – vegetable soup! Jimmy looked at Staff Nurse; Staff Nurse looked back at Jimmy; they both turned to look – hard – at Katie.

"Well, she led you up the garden path, all right," said Sister Beckwith, when Katie explained the incident. "But only because you didn't read her notes. Elderly patients must be kept upright as much as possible. Can you think why?"

Privately, Katie thought it was just to keep the beds neat and tidy all day, but she knew she daren't suggest this to Sister, whose motto was always "patients first".

"Well, er…" Katie remembered the time when her gran had been in hospital. She was always grumbling about being forced to get up out of bed, to get dressed, to walk with her zimmer, to fetch her own cups of tea. Until, that is, she was allowed back home, when she was glad to be so mobile so soon. "To make them independent?" she suggested.

"Mrs Royston is not going to be very independent after a fall at ninety-three, now is she?" Sister gave the sort of long-suffering sigh guaranteed to make Katie feel stupid. She did. "No," Sister went on, "there's always a chance of pneumonia if old people lie in bed; and an old lady's limbs are stiff and frail – she's more likely to shift them about a bit when she's sitting up in a chair."

"But she only wanted to go for a nap," protested Katie. "My gran…"

"Your gran is not my patient," Sister cut in. "Maudie Royston would stay in bed all day if we let her. And then she'd never eat and it would…" She didn't need to continue.

Be the death of her, Katie thought, feeling like a murderer. She swallowed hard and waited for Sister's next onslaught.

It came. "*And* you moved her without help. You know that there must always be two people to move a patient, don't you?"

Katie flushed and looked at the wall behind Sister's desk. "Yes, Sister," she mumbled.

"It's for your own safety as well as the patient's. Nurses are cursed with back problems." Sister Beckwith sighed again and stretched her own lean back, as if to ease it.

She seemed to have finished so Katie nodded. "Yes, Sister. Sorry, Sister. Is that all?" she said.

"Not quite, Katie, just listen for a moment longer, if you please." Sister Beckwith leaned forward and spoke softly, confidentially. "Some of our patients are old, a few are rather confused, and the fact that you wear a uniform means you are a nurse – to them. But you are not – not yet. You can listen to their comments, sympathize with their grievances, soothe and comfort them where you can." She paused. "But you cannot take any decisions regarding their welfare. Is that clear?"

"Yes, Sister." Katie nodded, humbly. But inside she was furious! Not with Maudie, who she still thought of as "Miss Royston" – she rather admired her for getting her own way like that – but with herself. How could she have let the old dear con her?

As if reading her thoughts, Sister nodded. "Well, Maudie is a very independent lady – you'll just have to watch out for her tricks in future." She smiled, her sharp blue eyes twinkling behind little gold glasses. "Just because she's frail and old doesn't mean she doesn't have a mind of her own, you know." Katie was relieved to see the smile, even though she knew the joke was on herself. Just wait till she saw that Miss Royston again!

When she did, Maudie apologized in her utterly charming way and smilingly promised to be "a good girl". And at least Katie had learned not to believe her!

The second blunder was not so easily pushed aside. Both Katie and Nick Bone had been invited to join the Centenary Celebrations Committee – but he didn't suggest they go to it together, she noticed. Well, let him keep his superior distance, she didn't care!

On the afternoon of the meeting, her biology lecture ran late and she lost her way in the admin block. Five minutes … ten… Katie rushed down corridors and up flights of steps, frantically searching for Committee Room 3. When she eventually found it, she slipped in, muttered an apology and scuttled to the nearest vacant seat, a tall, wooden armchair, at the imposing circular table.

The speaker went on talking about financial matters as Katie stared down at the table, breathed deeply and tried to calm herself. Suddenly she became aware of silence. All around the table eyes were directed at her. And beyond her. Katie followed their gaze round to the back of her chair.

Where Mr Lester-Ellis stood staring down at her! He said nothing, his face set and stern, his blue eyes cold. Katie was frozen to the chair with embarrassment: why was everyone waiting? And what were they waiting for?

It was Nick Bone who rescued her.

"There's a seat over here," he said, softly, pulling out a spare (plastic) chair alongside himself.

Realizing at last that everyone was waiting for Mr Lester-Ellis to take *his* place, Katie grabbed her cloak and her bag and scuttled round to the other side of the table. Mr Lester-Ellis took his seat, the speaker resumed his speech and Katie heard nothing. She sat in a haze of figures and percentages, aware of nothing except her own stupidity.

So that when the Chair welcomed the first-year student reps and called for their progress reports, Katie was not at all prepared. And even before she could scramble to her feet, Nick Bone stood up. Speaking with the sort of quiet authority Katie never quite achieved, he gave a brief summary of the Tuesday meeting, implying that there was a wealth of talent at Kelham House, just waiting to be tapped, and assuring the committee that a financial estimate would be forthcoming.

The Chair was impressed. "Thank you, Mr ... er ... that was most interesting. Sister Thomas has obviously inspired the Kelham students with her own enthusiasm, as usual." She beamed, several committee members nodded thoughtfully, and Nick Bone sat down with a modest smile.

Katie could have wept! Hating him for rescuing her, hating herself for being so rushed and unprepared, she felt she wanted nothing more to do with the Centenary Committee. She'd resign right after the meeting, she vowed. If Nick Bone wanted to take everything over – well, let him!

Then Mr Lester-Ellis spoke. Shaking his shaggy head, he made it quite clear what he thought of the celebrations.

"There is more than enough to do just to keep this hospital running smoothly," he said, "and nothing to spare for trivia!" He glared all round the table and waited for his words to sink in. "I wish my opposition to be noted. But I shall remain on the committee – just to strike a note of sanity now and then." He sat down, leaned back in the carved wooden armchair, and glared up the table at a dark, plump woman, who, to Katie's amazement – and envy – smiled back at him quite calmly.

The Chair hastily thanked Mr Lester-Ellis for his comments and went on to introduce the next item. Katie, mentally and emotionally exhausted by now, gave up any attempt to follow. She sat quite still, letting it all flow over her, startled when people pushed chairs back and began to move.

"Well, that was very interesting, wasn't it?" Nick Bone observed at the end.

"Was it?" Katie felt that she should be thanking him, but before she had collected her thoughts, he moved off, chatting easily with the plump brunette who'd out-faced Mr Lester-Ellis. Sighing at her own ineptitude, Katie stood up ready to make her escape.

But she had to pass the high wooden chair by the door – and Mr Lester-Ellis, who interrupted his conversation to look hard at her, as if to memorize the features of the student who stole his place.

Well, he'd recognize her when he next saw her, she thought. And then she groaned: that would be next Wednesday – Mr Lester-Ellis's ward round, which she was already ordered to attend!

Chapter 4

The following Tuesday evening Katie sat in Kelham common room surrounded by five empty chairs. She was too early for the meeting but she wanted to be in her place before the others arrived, or at least, before Nick Bone arrived.

How was she going to handle this meeting? What would she do if Nick Bone took over, just as he had at the committee meeting? When the common room door opened, Katie clasped her clipboard tensely and waited for him to stride in. Trust him to arrive early too, just to suss out the ground.

But the door clicked quietly and Katie looked up to see Nikki Browne gliding across the carpet towards her.

"Oh, er, Katie, am I too early?" Nikki stood

nervously smoothing down her skirt, which was of some soft, dark material, shot through with shafts of vivid colour, like a stained glass window.

"No, not at all – sit yourself down!" Katie heard her Yorkshire accent coming out strongly. Why did Nikki always have this effect on her? She made her feel like an oik, a country cousin or something. She was so cool, so quiet and controlled. Even producing coffee in the landing kitchen, she put out the mugs on a tray, with her own little leather mats underneath to catch the drips.

Nikki settled herself on a high-backed chair and crossed her ankles neatly. "I'm so glad to catch you here on your own," she said. "I'd like a private word with you, if I may?"

"Of course," said Katie, surprised that this apparently superior girl was requesting something of her.

"You see…" Nikki hesitated. "I'm not sure I can contribute anything to this, er, show idea…"

"Well, we've got to," said Katie, groaning again at her own bluntness.

"Yes, I do see that." Nikki blinked rapidly, silky lashes over her pale blue eyes. "But I mean what if one just can't?"

"Oh, come on, Nikki, everyone can do something. We're not producing a West End show, are we?"

"But, d'you see, I can't do anything in that line. I don't play an instrument, I can't sing, or dance, or

… or … anything!" She looked earnestly at Katie, her lip trembling, eyes gleaming with tears. "I simply couldn't face an audience – not ever!"

Katie looked at her in amazement and for a moment she felt quite sorry for her. But before she could say anything, in came Barbara, pulling Jan Buczowski along by the arm.

"I found this young man almost skulking at the door," she grinned. "That's right, isn't it, Jan? That's what you were doing?"

"Pardon?" asked the bewildered boy.

"Skulking – outside the door," Barbara repeated, slowly.

"Skulking – interesting word." Jan looked as though he was making a mental note of it. "I was waiting, actually," he explained to Katie.

Sometimes his accent is so correct he sounds as classy as Nikki, she thought. "You could have come on in," she told him. "This is the common room – you know – common to all of us. It's yours as well as ours."

Before Jan could ask about that new word, Claire breezed in. "Sorry I'm late an' all," she said cheerily. "Though I see I'm not the last."

They all looked round and noted Nick Bone's absence.

"Well, it's just about seven," said Katie, rather relieved that she was left in charge. "So let's get going, shall we?"

"Well, now." Barbara flipped through some papers on her clipboard. "I've found out a bit about finances. We can get money from two sources – the Centenary fund, and the Students' Entertainment fund."

"Well done, Barbara!" Katie congratulated her. "Do we know how much?"

"Not until we come up with some projected figures."

"Ah, I see I've arrived just in time!" Nick Bone spoke from the doorway. "Hi, everyone – I'm not late, am I?"

"You said you were just in time," Barbara reminded him.

"To discuss finances – yes." Nick picked up a hard-backed chair and placed it neatly opposite Katie. "There's quite a bit of money around for this celebration," he went on. "I think we'll be able to get just about anything we want – provided we can account for it."

"But surely we'll be needing very little if all we're doing is singing the odd folk-song, playing a bit of music – you know?" Claire said.

Katie saw her chance – and for once she took it. "Well, actually, I've had an idea…" And, speaking rapidly without looking in Nick Bone's direction, she outlined the cabaret plan to them all. "We could even turn the whole room into a nightclub, you see," she went on. "Get the students to act as waiters, er, and so on." Katie suddenly wondered how many of the nursing students would be willing to play nightclub girls.

"Hey – that's great!" said Barbara. "You know, I thought this was going to be some sort of folksy get-together so I didn't dare suggest it, but I'm a bit of a singer myself – blues, jazz, that sort of thing."

"Really?" Katie added Barbara's offer to her list. "Any other ideas?" She looked round, still avoiding Nick Bone's eyes.

But it was he who spoke. "If you're following the cabaret theme, you'll need a Master of Ceremonies, who could double as stage-manager," he suggested. "To keep the whole thing running."

"I've already thought of that." Katie couldn't help the hard tone in her voice; this smarmy-charmy bloke really got up her nose! "I'll combine it with producing."

Nick shrugged. "Don't you think you're taking rather a lot on?"

"You think I can't cope?" she said, sharply.

"I don't know what *you're* capable of," he said, quietly. "But I do know *I've* got enough on, this term, without trying to prove I'm Andrew Lloyd Webber. I know my limitations – I've run the ship's disco, karaoke and games nights for years. I'll front your show – no sweat."

Nobody spoke. Katie stared straight ahead, feeling as if she and Nick were involved in some kind of power struggle. "I don't know what *you're* capable of," he'd said. Right – she'd show him!

"I'm quite capable of getting this show together and keeping it running on the night," she said. Then she paused, realizing too late how egotistical that sounded. She'd better offer Nick another rôle…

But before she came up with one, he stood up. "Well, if you can manage it all by yourself, I suggest you get on with it."

He pushed back his chair and strode out.

"He is upset," observed Jan.

"What the hell did you do that for?" Barbara asked Katie.

"I didn't mean…" Katie muttered.

Everyone was silent. Katie looked round at them miserably. Failed again, Katie Harding, she thought. How many times had Dad warned her about her quick tongue? Well, it wasn't quick enough just then; she couldn't think how to continue the meeting.

Rescue came from an unexpected quarter. "If you don't mind…?" Nikki Browne spoke, hesitantly as usual. "May I?" she asked Katie.

"Please do!" Katie hoped she spoke humbly.

"It's just that I have a fiddle – I thought it might be useful – for Jan, d'you see."

"You have – where?" Clare asked eagerly.

"Here – it's just been delivered from home. Shall I get it?"

"Of course. Hey, Jan, you hear that?" Claire almost hugged the bewildered boy. "A fiddle – you understand – your violin – we can start rehearsing!"

When Nikki came back with the instrument, Jan took it out of its case, carefully at first, then, as he looked more closely, he held it up almost reverently.

"This is yours?" he asked Nikki.

She shook her head. "It's been in the family – you know – quite a time." She gave him a quick, nervous smile. "My mother – she used to play – and my brother at one time, but…" she paused.

"It is a beautiful instrument," pronounced Jan, solemnly. "I cannot be responsible…"

"Oh, but yes… I mean do… It's insured and anyway I know you'll take care…" Nikki looked earnestly at Jan and flushed.

"But if it is stolen, or er, damaged?"

"I'm sure you'll look after it," said Nikki, more firmly now. "It's my little gesture – you know – I'm hopeless at anything – can't dance, can't sing – like, er, Nick – but well, at least I've helped a bit…"

The pause was made more awkward by her reference to Nick Bone.

"Well, Jan, aren't you going to try it?" asked Claire, brightly.

And Jan did try, tentatively at first, but steadily growing in confidence as he felt his way into the instrument, from a simple folk melody to wild gypsy dances that had the girls tapping and clapping. Even

Nikki was joining in, off the beat, perhaps, but relaxed and flushed and almost happy.

But, as usual, Katie's glow of achievement was short-lived.

"Well, we've made a start," Barbara observed later, as she, Claire and Katie sat drinking coffee in the kitchen upstairs. Nikki, at Jan's insistence, had gone with him to lock the violin into her room. And they hadn't come back for coffee.

"A bad start, I'm afraid," groaned Katie.

"Yeah, you certainly got across friend Nick right enough," Barbara grinned.

"I didn't mean to. It was just – well, after that episode at the committee meeting, I had the feeling he was going to take everything over…"

"And you wanted to be the one to do that," finished Barbara.

"No!" Katie was most indignant. "I just had an idea I wanted us to develop – together."

"But we will need some kind of co-ordinator," said Claire, softly. "And you know, you have got a lot on – you're on the committee and all."

"I'll give up the committee, then."

"No, don't do that. We need someone on that committee, it's where we'll get extra money, support, publicity – all kinds of help," said Barbara.

"Well, Nick Bone's on it."

"But he's not going to be looking out for us if he's

not involved in the cabaret," Claire pointed out.

Katie groaned. "Oh, blast my big mouth! I've let you all down, haven't I?"

"No, Katie – you've got us all going, that's what you've done." Claire smiled and pushed a tin box across the table. "Now, you just nibble one of Da's ginger cookies, guaranteed to settle the mind," she smiled.

"Take two," suggested Barbara. "And maybe your mind will settle on a plan to get Nick Bone back into the cabaret!"

But the cookies didn't work and, after a restless night, Katie reported to Porchester Ward feeling utterly useless.

"About as useful as a chocolate poker," her dad would have told her. And just then, she'd have had to agree. Not only had she upset a useful member of the Kelham Six, but here she was, the tail end of Mr Lester-Ellis's entourage, ignored by everyone, the lowest form of hospital life. Katie stifled a yawn and wondered yet again if she was right for the job.

Mr Lester-Ellis consulted files and X-rays and, occasionally, his registrar or Sister Beckwith. The two junior doctors, the physiotherapist, the occupational therapist, Staff Nurse Howe and Student Nurse Jimmy Ashbey just followed on, occasionally smiling or nodding wisely. The remainder of the staff tried hard to keep out of the way and as for

Katie – Mr Lester-Ellis hadn't even glanced in her direction, she thought indignantly.

But he was quite a different person on the ward round, she noticed. Moving softly, murmuring gently, he often paused to chat to his patients – many of whom had no idea what a distinguished visitor he was.

Maudie, as usual, had her own opinion.

"Well, Miss Royston, are you quite comfortable?" Mr Lester-Ellis knew Maudie's case so well by now he scarcely needed to check her notes. Katie noted with satisfaction that he, too, addressed the old lady formally.

Miss Royston glanced up from her crossword. "I'd be more comfortable in bed," she remarked.

"Ah, but you'd be less healthy," he rejoined.

"At ninety-three one can hardly hope for perfect health," she pointed out.

"No, but we like to keep you up to the mark."

"What for?"

There was a slight pause. Katie held her breath.

"Because that's our job," answered Mr Lester-Ellis quietly.

The old lady looked steadily at him and nodded. "And you do it very well, my dear," she agreed. "Is it time for our morning coffee?"

Katie grinned broadly as she passed Maudie's bed and joined the entourage just in time to hear Mr Lester-Ellis suggest that Miss Royston should rest on her bed for an hour in the afternoons if she wanted to.

And Katie was very satisfied to find him prescribing her own "treatment". She could hardly say "I told you so" to Sister Beckwith so she contented herself with staring hard at Jimmy, who looked up from his notebook and winked at her!

That morning seemed to Katie to be a turning-point in her ward training. It wasn't just that she'd been instinctively right about Maudie's rest-time, though that had given her a glow of pleasure, it was when they all turned to leave and she was suddenly face to face with Mr Lester-Ellis.

Mr Lester-Ellis bent and fixed Katie with a piercing gaze from under his craggy brows. Everyone stood still; even the patients were silent.

"Ah! New student, eh?"

"That's right, Mr Lester-Ellis," Sister Beckwith agreed.

"Shaping up well?"

"It's early days," said Sister Beckwith. But she said it with a smile at Katie.

"Humph." Mr Lester-Ellis moved closer. "Seem to know you from somewhere," he said. "What's your name?"

Katie dug deep and found her voice. "Student Nurse Katie Harding, sir," she said.

He nodded, a half-smile flickering around his lips. "Well, Katie Harding, you may feel like a very little cog in this huge machine of a hospital, but don't forget what little cogs do!"

He moved past her abruptly and the others followed him out of the ward. Little cog Katie stood in a daze until a call from Eileen, the auxiliary nurse, roused her. She needed Katie's help to lift a back patient up on to his pillows.

"I know you're not supposed to be an extra pair of hands," Eileen apologized, "but you can see how everybody else's occupied."

"That's all right," said Katie. "I'd rather work than stand about watching."

"I know," Eileen said. "But watching's important. Just watch how I take hold of Harold's shoulder, then take his other one in the same way – ready?"

Together they gently lifted the patient up on to his pillows.

"Thanks, Eileen, that's very comfortable – and it didn't hurt my back at all," said Harold. "And thanks to you too, Nurse!"

And Katie smiled at the old man, resting now on his pillows. Nurse! Perhaps one day, with a lot of watching and a lot of waiting and some very hard work, she might even live up to the title!

Bending now to collect the sheets and towels for the laundry, Katie suddenly felt happy. And she remembered what small cogs had to do – they had to work together with the bigger cogs and so move the whole machine.

Better a small cog than a chocolate poker, she grinned to herself. I'll just have to work harder to keep the Kelham Six running smoothly. And that includes Nick Bone!

Chapter 5

Weekends were a bit of a problem for Katie. College was closed, Kelham half empty and she'd agreed with Dad that travelling home was too expensive. Gary's letters urged her to come to the match, for a day's walking or a party, but it all seemed so far away now; she wasn't sure she wanted to be a part of Gary's life again. And anyway, she had plenty of work to do: notes to copy up, background reading, her ward diary – and the cabaret script.

This seemed much more urgent than any of the others – and much more difficult. Katie tore yet another page from her A4 pad, scrunched it up into a ball and flung it across the room. It was no use writing sketches until she knew who could act in them.

Dejected, she went along the corridor to make herself a coffee. Alone on Saturday night, she reflected, thinking of the gang back home getting ready to live it up at the local wine bar. At the top of the stairs she hesitated, wondering whether to go down and ring Gary, just to hear the sound of his voice, the latest gossip. As she paused she sniffed, aware of a spicy-sweet smell drifting along the corridor.

Barbara looked out of the kitchen door. "Hi, Katie – just in time to sample a bowl of my new chowder." In spite of her glamorous looks and her laid-back attitude, Barbara was one of the few students who cooked real meals in that kitchen. Others might open up a tin or a pizza – Barbara peeled and chopped and sliced fresh vegetables, steaming, stir-frying, simmering, and producing pungent stews with mysteriously spicy flavours.

Katie followed her nose. "I was just going to have a coffee," she said, standing at the kitchen door.

Barbara threw her a shrewd glance. "You look as if you could do with something a bit stronger," she said. "Anything wrong?"

Katie sighed. "No, not really," she said. "Just a bit – you know, fed up."

Barbara ladled a steaming golden stream into one of her vast blue bowls. "There you go!" she said, pushing it over in Katie's direction.

"Are you sure?" Katie sat down now at the table and picked up a spoon.

"No – I'll take it back," threatened Barbara, "if you don't get on with it." She poured a second bowl and sat at the table opposite Katie.

They sipped their soup in silence for a moment, then Katie, relaxed now, sat back. "You're a terrific cook, Barbara. Why don't you give up nursing and open a restaurant?"

Barbara's dark eyes shone. "Don't think the idea has not been long in my mind," she said.

"But…?" Katie prompted.

"But have you ever tried to raise capital from the bank?"

Katie shook her head. She knew Dad had enough trouble over the mortgage on their little terraced house, without either of them going in for bank loans.

"You know how many restaurants go bust in any week?" Barbara persisted.

Again, Katie shook her head.

"Sister, you doan' know nuthin'!" Barbara wagged her finger at Katie, like a wise old Caribbean granny.

Katie sighed. "You're right," she agreed. "Sometimes I think I've never really lived. I mean," she took another slurp of soup, "look at the rest of you – Jan escaping a civil war, Claire from the edges of another. Nikki Browne from the higher echelons of society and you with your exotic background…"

"If you think Brixton is exotic, lady, then you certainly haven't lived."

"It is to me. I've only ever been to London once."

"Where did you go?"

"Houses of Parliament – on a demo with Dad."

"Hey, well, talk about exotic!" said Barbara. "What were you marching for?"

"Jobs." Katie sighed, depressed again.

There was a silence for a moment as they bent to drink their soup.

"I know what you need," Barbara said. "Why don't you come over to the doctors' mess tonight?"

"The what?"

"Oh, come on, Katie, where've you been this past month? You mean you've never heard of the sizzling night-life of St Ag's?"

"I thought it was in the pub down the road." Katie had been down there with Claire, but, appalled by the cost of even an orange juice, she hadn't gone again.

"No, there's a much better scene right here – for free, almost. No entrance fee, cheap drinks, even the occasional rich medic who'll treat you – if you're lucky!"

Katie hesitated. She did have some money saved, vaguely thinking it would do for train fare back home if she ever succumbed to Gary's pressing invitations.

"Come on," Barbara urged. "It's only quiet early on, until the rugger crowd get in, but a bit of company will do you good."

Well, Katie reflected, Gary was very probably on his way out to find a bit of company right now. Why shouldn't she do the same? "OK," she agreed. "Let's go!"

Katie had imagined the doctors' mess to be rather like a gentlemen's club – all red leather and plush with perhaps a fire roaring in a vast, stone hearth, and a hushed atmosphere where conversation was whispered and secrets passed on. Now, she saw she'd been wrong; Kelham House common room had more signs of gracious living than St Ag's junior doctors' mess. Still, the bar was brightly lit, the vinyl seating comfortable and the juke-box well stacked, and on a platform at the end stood an alarming array of electronics – presumably for bands or discos. Some of it might prove useful for the cabaret show, Katie noted as she sat back and waited for Barbara to bring the first drinks.

She took her time; Katie could see the two glasses up on the bar awaiting collection, but every time Barbara moved to get them, someone called her or came up to talk. Katie was amazed how many people seemed to know her. Even when she finally picked up their drinks and started across the room, someone waved to her. It was Nick Bone, Katie noticed – and with a rather plump brunette who looked vaguely familiar.

"Who's that with Nick Bone?" she asked Barbara, rather casually.

Barbara didn't even need to check. "I thought you knew her," she said. "Tina Brookes must be on every committee in the hospital – she's the co-ordinator of all the centenary celebrations."

Katie nodded. Of course, that's where she'd seen her – smiling calmly back at the irate Lester-Ellis at that first Centenary Committee meeting. She blushed even now to think of it.

"Have you said anything to Nick yet?" Barbara asked.

"What about?" Katie asked, innocently.

"About coming back into the fold – to MC the cabaret."

"How can I? He's totally ignored me since that meeting."

"Not surprising, after the way you treated him," Barbara laughed. "Look, I know you've got no time for each other, but with only six Kelhamites, we are going to need him."

"We can do it without an MC and I can stage-manage," said Katie.

"Yes," agreed Barbara. "We can even do it without music, scenery – money – but it'll not be a success. And I'm not giving my time and talent to a flop, Katie Harding, so you'd better start building a few bridges – like now, this very evening. Excuse me – I'm needed."

Katie watched Barbara walk across to the platform, where someone was fumbling about fixing up a keyboard. She walked like a queen, Katie thought, head high, back straight, looking at least six feet tall, though she was only average height.

And she was right. Katie knew they needed a Master of Ceremonies – it was the leading part in the whole enterprise, and Nick Bone was ideal for it. So it was up to her to "build bridges", as Barbara put it. But how? She glanced across to the corner table where Nick and Tina sat, deep in intimate conversation. For a moment Katie had a glimpse of Gary and herself, sitting in the local wine bar, waiting for the rest of the gang to turn up, saying nothing because they'd known each other so long there was nothing left to say…

"…*a little bit funny*…" sang a light, smoky voice, backed by a very expert keyboard player. Katie stared at the platform – and saw that the singer was Barbara. She'd removed her jacket to reveal a simple, clinging, little black dress and was holding a hand-mike up to her shining red mouth as if she was about to eat it rather than sing into it.

Katie was transfixed. Barbara had casually offered to sing a song or two in the cabaret, as if to fill the occasional gap. But she was a star! Katie forgot her drink, forgot Gary, Nick Bone, even the cabaret script, as she gave herself up to the bitter-sweet sound of Barbara's voice.

She was back after three songs, walking through the applause, nodding graciously, smiling only slightly.

"Barbara – you never told us," Katie admonished.

"You never asked," Barbara reminded her.

"I asked for volunteers."

"Yeah, well, like I said, I thought the ethnic bit had got in first and there's one thing I'm not and that's ethnic."

"I think everyone's an ethnic something," said Katie.

"You think you're an ethnic Yorkshire lass, I suppose?"

"Eeh bah gum ah don't know abaht that but I do know tha's right champion, tha knaws," Katie mocked.

Barbara bowed her head in acknowledgement of the compliment. "Yes, well, cut out the ham acting for a moment and just listen to this young medic on the keys – I reckon we could use him."

So they sipped their drinks and watched a small, round, bespectacled young man coaxing pure jazz piano sounds out of the electronic keyboard.

"Would you mind if I joined you?" The words jerked Katie out of her dream of the Kelham Kabaret Klub in a real nightclub setting: blue smoke, spotlight, MC and all. She looked up to see Tina Brookes's questioning face.

"Feel free!" Barbara drew out another stool. "We

thought you were otherwise engaged," she added ironically.

"Well, it was Nick who said I should speak to – Katie Harding, isn't it?" She sat down, rather heavily, and smiled at Katie.

Katie nodded.

"Tina Brookes – co-ordinator of the centenary celebrations." Her face lit up with a wide smile. "And Nick tells me that you're the dynamo behind the first-year revue."

Katie flushed. Could Nick Bone have said that about her?

"Oh, I'm just producing Kelham's bit," she said.

And at that moment Nick Bone joined them. "Anyone for a drink?" he asked, smiling all round but avoiding Katie's startled look.

"Oh, yes, look – you get us a drink while Katie tells me all her plans," Tina suggested.

The piano was silent now and Barbara slipped away to capture the medical musician while Katie told Tina about the cabaret plan.

"It's brilliant!" Tina announced when Nick came back with the drinks. "There's so much scope…"

Nick put the glasses on the table.

"Thank you very much," muttered Katie as he passed her one.

"Pleasure," he said smoothly, taking over Barbara's stool, close up to Tina.

Tina didn't seem to notice; she was too busy talking to Katie.

"The only thing that's bothering me right now – well, among three thousand others, of course – is the contributions from the rest of the first-years."

Katie's heart sank. What if the others were going to do something so wonderful that the Kelham cabaret would be a flop? She remembered Barbara's warning.

"What do you mean?" she asked.

"Well, I know that Walton House have got a brilliant little play but it lasts only fifteen minutes, and Bingham haven't even got started. And then, it's so difficult for the non-residents to get together. Some of them are mature students – wives, husbands, mothers, fathers – they have so many other responsibilities. On the other hand, we do want them to feel included…"

"So?" Katie was unusually cautious. She thought she knew what was coming but she wanted to make sure. No more foolish blunders in front of these two, she prayed.

"Well, with your cabaret idea, you could rehearse all the main acts with the residents, including Walton's health-farm play and anything Bingham can come up with. Then you use the day students as extras in the nightclub – as cloakroom attendants, cigarette girls – you know the kind of thing. They'll need very little rehearsal and yet they'll feel included in the project. No?" She beamed from Nick to Katie.

"Yes!" they answered together, and for a moment their eyes met, his amused, hers startled. Katie blushed and dropped her glance to her drink.

"There's only one snag," Tina went on.

"Which is?" asked Katie.

"You!" she replied, smiling broadly at Katie's dismay. "You see, my dear, you're a first-year student with a full college timetable. You're already serving on the Centenary Committee, and now I'm asking you to produce the whole first-year show. It really is too much, you know."

She paused as if waiting for one or other of them to speak.

Katie swallowed hard and looked straight at Nick Bone. "I can do it," she said. "But I'll need an MC – and a stage manager – and," she went on more firmly, now, "somebody who can keep everyone in order…" She stopped and looked deep into her cider once more.

"Yeah, I can see that." Nick spoke casually, as if the idea was new. He turned to Tina. "I told you I used to run the show on the ship – a bit of disco, karaoke, quizzes and games. I think I could keep things moving on the night, get the audience going, keep it all in order. But this is Katie's idea – she should be in charge – all right with you, Katie?" He turned the full sharp blue of his gaze back to her.

And Katie, unusually stuck for words, nodded.

"Well, that's settled then." Tina Brookes beamed at both of them. "You know, I sometimes think I get more work done in here on a Saturday night than we ever do in committee." Her voice faded as a loud – and very unmusical – song cut through the air. "Ah – yes – the return of the Rugby team." Tina waved across to the bar. "I need to corner them. Excuse me – see you at the next meeting…"

She picked up her glass and made her way over to the noisy group of very large young men who had obviously already consumed a large number of pints.

"Tina Brookes is the only woman I know who would go out of her way to corner the Rugby team," Nick observed. "She's even more indefatigable than you are!"

"Me?" Katie was too surprised to be embarrassed.

"Yeah – you're a glutton for work, aren't you? This is the first time I've seen you socializing since we started here."

"Yes, well, I've had a lot on, you know, and…"

"And you've got a boyfriend back home," Nick finished.

She stared at him angrily. Just when she thought they were getting on so well he had to spoil it. Spoil what?

"I was going to say I haven't got much money for socializing," she said, defiantly.

"Well, most people haven't," he agreed. "You don't have to drink all evening here, you know. Half of cider, cup of coffee – nobody objects if you have only the one."

"Yes, well, now I know, don't I?" Katie was still angry – with herself as much as with Nick. How did he always manage to put her in the wrong? She sipped her cider slowly, silently, until, to her relief, Barbara returned.

"I see you two have been making it up while I've been away!" she smiled. "This is Theo – our accompanist."

Theo blinked through his glasses and nodded all round, accepted a drink from Nick and listened to Katie's plans. Katie liked him from the start; he took them seriously, put a few suggestions in and assured her that he'd never miss a rehearsal – except when he was on nights. Then he took Barbara off to the platform again and the other two lingered over their drinks, listening to smooth, blue music.

People started dancing – not disco but shuffling round the floor, close together. Old-fashioned, thought Katie, scornfully.

"Dance?"

She jumped. "What?"

"I asked you if you'd like to dance," Nick Bone repeated.

"Well, er, I … I can't. Not this stuff."

"Ah, I see." He glanced at his watch. "Well, the

disco starts in ten minutes. If you'll excuse me I'll indulge my old-fashioned preference for dancing with a partner." And he was gone. The next time she saw him he was dancing very smoothly, very close to Tina Brookes, who obviously shared his "old-fashioned" tastes.

Katie watched their graceful, matching steps, heard Barbara's voice sweeping high, dipping low, and suddenly she realized that Tina Brookes's idea was great. There'd be plenty of mature students who could dance like that – they could be part of the club and part of the audience, and the audience could join in, after the cabaret. Katie had a sudden vision of Mr Lester-Ellis smooching with Sister Beckwith and giggled to herself. Well, that might be fantasy, but first thing Monday morning she would be chatting to the non-res students – the ones she normally never noticed! Her fingers itched to get going with lists and plans.

The soft, sweet music ended, the disco beat took over and, amazingly, Nick Bone returned to ask her to dance. For the next hour or so, Katie Harding forgot all about her cabaret!

It was past midnight when she came back to her room. Humming happily, she picked the scrunched-up papers from the floor and glanced at the A4 pad on the bedside table. Too late to start work again now, she thought, her mind would be clearer in the morning. She undressed and washed quickly, and snuggled under her quilt. Tired, but happy, she thought, remembering Dad's bedtime stories from years ago. Well, her evening out had cheered her up. And it had solved two of her problems: the cabaret and Nick Bone's part in it.

The smile faded. Come to think of it, she wasn't sure whether Nick Bone was a solution or a problem!

Chapter 6

And now, the only problem with weekends was that there weren't enough of them. Days passsed, weeks passed, and Katie had no time to be homesick; phone calls home were hurried, letters to Gary briefer and rarer. Every waking minute of every day and evening was filled – mainly, it must be admitted, with her work on the cabaret.

She soon found a hidden wealth of talent amongst the day students: a couple of ex-miners who did a great comedy double-act; a juggler and a magician called Marlene Majinski – day-name Maureen Major; a Welsh student with a marvellous tenor voice; and a few good amateur actors just waiting for Katie's scripts. As word got round, other people came with offers of help with the lighting, props and costumes and were soon pressed into appearing as extras in the "nightclub".

All this cost her many cups of coffee, a lot of telephone calls and a great deal of time so she had to leave the rehearsals of the Kelham acts to Nick Bone.

"Thought you didn't like him?" Claire said, a few weeks later, as they walked over to lectures.

"Well, he's a bit of a slime, don't you think?" Katie said. "He always makes me feel as if I'm blundering about making a fool of myself when he's around."

"What do you mean, 'when he's around'?" Claire teased. "I thought that's what you did all the time?"

"Thank you, fans, I love you too!" Katie made a mock bow. "And anyway, I'm sure he's doing a great job – don't know where I'd be without him…"

"Getting up to date on your project?" Claire reminded her.

Katie groaned. Her project was about fractures – causes, effects and treatments, linked with her observations on the Orthopaedic ward. So far it consisted merely of scribbled notes and a few markers in her anatomy text book – and it was due in during the following week.

"You must get on with it, you know," Claire said, gently.

"I know, I know – don't nag me!" said Katie. "I've got enough to worry about with the cabaret."

"The cabaret won't qualify you as a nurse."

Katie wasn't even sure whether she cared about that. "I've got this marvellous idea for a series of comedy sketches showing a history of medicine through the ages," she explained. "I've thought of some great scenes. Did you know that prehistoric people did brain surgery?"

Claire shuddered. "And that's supposed to be funny?" she asked.

"It will be when I've written it," Katie laughed.

"You should be writing your project, not funny sketches," said Claire.

"I'll do that at the weekend," Katie promised. "Clear the way for the real work."

"Katie, nursing is our real work, you know." Claire pushed open the door to the lecture room.

Katie sighed. "You sound just like my dad," she said. She brightened at the thought. "Anyway, there's always the Easter break."

Rushing through the day in a flurry of names and lists and hurried auditions with prospective performers, Katie was aware of Claire's reminder – and of the guilt she felt about the neglected project. Dad would be disappointed in her, she knew; he despised skivers.

"This weekend," she promised herself. And she even went so far as to borrow a few useful books from Claire – anatomy this time, not drama.

When she got back to Kelham House late on

Friday afternoon, there was a letter awaiting her. Katie's heart sank as she recognized Gary's handwriting. That was another problem she must do something about, with the Easter vacation coming up. But she just flung the letter with her cloak on to the bed and sat down at her desk to examine the anatomy books. To her surprise, she found them very interesting; she reached for her pad and began to make notes. Kelham, the cabaret and Gary's letter all faded, as she concentrated on her work.

"Katie Harding! Katie Harding – telephone!" Someone was hammering at her door. Katie looked up, dazed.

"What?" she asked.

"There's a phone call for you – from a call box. Be quick!"

As she rushed downstairs to the foyer, Katie pulled her thoughts together. It was probably one of the day students trying to back out of a part in the cabaret, she thought. Damn! That meant more searching… She picked up the phone.

"Hi – Katie Harding," she said, trying to sound cool and professional rather than breathless.

"Katie – didn't you get my letter?"

It was Gary.

Katie felt as if the wind had been knocked out of her. "Hi – hello, Gary," she said, weakly.

"Katie – you all right?"

"Yes… It's a long way to run to the phone."

73

"Did you get my letter?" he repeated.

"Yes I did – just now –"

"So what are you going to do?"

Katie took a deep breath and shook her head, like someone coming up from a deep dive. "Do?" she asked, playing for time. Presumably Gary had written to ask her to come to some party or other at Easter. "I'm not sure," she said. "I've got a lot of work on." Well, that much was true anyway.

There was silence at the other end. "Gary?" she said. "Are you still there?"

"Yes, I'm here," he choked. "And my money's running out. Katie – have you read my letter?"

"Er, well, I've only just got back," she hedged.

"Go and read it, and ring me back." For once, he sounded quite commanding.

"Whcre? Where are you?" she asked.

"On my way home. Ring me there…" The line went dead. His money was gone.

Katie replaced the instrument and stood gazing at it, puzzled. "On my way home," Gary had said. But from where? And why hadn't he waited to ring her from home? And why had he sounded so upset when she'd told him about her holiday work? Something in the letter, he'd said. Well, she'd better go and read it before they spoke again. Sighing heavily, she plodded back upstairs.

"Katie – you have a moment?" Jan stood on the landing, Nikki's fiddle in his hand. "I have problems

– with the noise – people are complaining…" He pushed his glossy black fringe back with his bow hand, nervously. "But I must practise. Nick says you are coming to see the next rehearsal."

Katie nodded. "We'll have to find you a room away from all the others," she said. "What about the basement?"

"So I thought, too, but there is Mr Has… Haslan?"

Haslam was the caretaker who ruled the basement.

"I'll have a word with him," Katie promised.

"Right – we'll go now?" Jan asked.

Helplessly, Katie watched him descend the stairs. Something in Gary's voice made her want to open his letter immediately. Even if he had to cycle home from the phone box it wouldn't take him long. Nothing was far away in their village and he'd be waiting for her call…

"Katie – come now." Jan looked back at her, trusting her, relying on her to sort out his problem. She went back downstairs.

It took an hour to find Mr Haslam, clear out a corner of the basement, fix a new light bulb, and improvise a music stand out of an old bedside locker. Katie left the basement to the strains of an aching Balkan love lyric and plodded yet again upstairs.

Katie love, she read.

I've been ringing and ringing but nobody ever seems to find you. Apparently you're never in your room – or anywhere in the hostel these days. We'll just have to fix a time when you're near a phone – if you're interested enough to bother.

I'm writing because I think you should know your dad's not well. My mum called round when she hadn't seen him up the village for a few days and he looked really poorly, she said. Sick and dizzy. He thought it was just the 'flu but next thing we know he's taken off to the infirmary. For tests, they said. He wouldn't ring you – said you had too much on – but I think he'd like to see you, if only for a short visit. Can you get away this weekend?

Let me know your train times and I'll meet you. Maybe after you've been to see your dad we could go out somewhere? I think there's lots to talk about, don't you?

As ever, love,
Gary

Katie sat on her bed looking blankly at the wall. She read the letter again – and again. She couldn't believe it. Her dad, her live-wire, bustling, energetic dad, ill? He'd never had anything more than a strained muscle or two even in his heavy mining days. And now the pit was closed, he was one of the few ex-miners who was glad to have escaped without a bad chest.

"Poorer but healthier," he'd told her, when he knew the worst. "We'll have to live carefully, but simple food and fresh air never hurt anybody. And who knows? I might even live long enough to see you 'settled'!"

And Katie had laughed, slapped his shoulder and assured him she'd no plans to be "settled" for many years yet. "Settled", in their community meant only one thing – married with two-point-four kids. And Katie knew she didn't want to "settle" for that.

And now he was ill. "Tests", Gary had said. But what did that mean? And which department of the hospital was he in? Gary hadn't mentioned that. She was struck by a sudden thought. Perhaps Gary had even been at the infirmary when he'd rung. She looked at her watch and groaned; almost nine o'clock. They wouldn't welcome enquiries at that time of night. And anyway, she hadn't got the number, the ward, anything. Except Gary.

Down again, to the phone in the foyer.

"No panic," Gary told her. "He's just having these tests – for blood pressure, I think. Haematology is where he is – that's blood, isn't it?"

Katie took down the number of the infirmary. Gary hadn't thought to ask for the name of her dad's consultant, the ward sister – anyone. Just like everybody else, when faced with hospital, she reflected, take orders from anyone without asking even the simplest question.

"But have you seen him?"

"Oh, yes – I went with Mum tonight. Hey – I

drove all the way. Just waiting for a date for my test then I'll be able to come over to see you any time…"

"But how is he?" Katie interrupted.

"Oh, he looks a lot better, Mum said, now that he's resting. Fed up, of course, but you know your dad."

"Yes." But did she? Katie suddenly felt like a stranger, a foreigner to that past life in the sprawling pit village. She knew her old dad, her strength and her support, but not this dad, a sick man in hospital. She couldn't imagine the lively, fresh-faced man lying still and pale against the pillows.

"Are you sure he's all right?" she asked again. And when Gary had reassured her again she said that she'd come home on Saturday.

"I'll meet you. Come to us for dinner, then somebody can drive you over to the infirmary," Gary said. "So that's settled. There's a train gets in at 10.30. I'll be there. Right?"

It wasn't, but this was not the time for deep discussion. And anyway her money was running out. "Right," said Katie, and paused. "Well … er … 'bye," she said, eventually.

"Yeah – see you, then," he said. " 'Bye, Katie!"

So much for a working weekend, she thought, as she stacked Claire's books on the dressing-table. No point in trying to work now, it was too late and she was too worried about her father. And, she suddenly realized, she'd called a non-residents' audition on Sunday afternoon. How was she going to fit that in? She rushed out of the room and down the corridor to Nick Bone's room.

"Yeah – no sweat," Nick assured her when she explained. "Sorry about your dad, though." He looked at her, quizzically. "Close family, are you?"

Katie blushed. "There's only me and him," she said, simply.

Nick nodded. "Ah well, bound to be close, then," he said. "But don't worry before you know the facts," he said. "It's not unusual for people who've worked hard all their lives to have a bit of a collapse before they adjust to retirement."

Katie looked at him with new interest; he wasn't just bulling her up, he sounded really sympathetic. "But Dad always says he's glad to be out of the pit," she remembered.

"Well, he would, wouldn't he? Not to worry you, not to worry himself, most likely. I don't suppose there's any chance of another job?"

Katie shook her head. "Nearly fifty," she said. "Not a chance."

"Well, off you go and cheer the poor chap up." Nick flung an arm round her shoulder. "I'll see the day students for you – and tell you all about the likely ones later."

Katie's shoulder burned from his touch. "Thanks," she said as casually as she could. "I'll owe you one."

"And I'll claim it one of these days, Katie Harding – you just see if I don't!"

And Katie spent the whole of her train journey wondering what kind of favour Nick would claim from her – and hoping.

Chapter 7

"Katie! Over here!" She followed the call, heart sinking. This was only the first of a weekend full of problems. Should she greet Gary with a hug? A kiss, even? After all, they hadn't met for months and she owed him at least three letters.

But luckily he was in a hurry. "Make haste!" he said, taking the weekend bag she'd borrowed from Claire. "Dad's waiting with the car on a double yellow line."

They travelled in silence, Gary concentrating on his driving and Mr Ledbetter following his every manoeuvre carefully. Katie was relieved; she didn't feel like talking just then. She sat back and gazed out of the window. In the distance she could see the pit-head wheels stilled and silent like monuments to a past age. And the pit-tips were being levelled now, some already green with tough grass.

"Hepton Main's a golf-course now," Mr Ledbetter told her. "What a come-down!"

Katie thought it looked like a great improvement, but for once, she didn't argue. She just sat back and wished she'd gone straight up to the infirmary all by herself.

But Gary's mother had everything organized.

"Visiting's not till two," she greeted Katie. "So there's plenty of time for you to have some dinner – you look as if you could do with a good meal."

And Katie had to admit she was right. She'd missed both supper the previous night and breakfast that morning, so the coffee she'd had on the train was slurping alarmingly around her empty stomach. Well, at least she'd be able to do justice to Annie Ledbetter's famous pastry!

"More steak-and-kidney pie, Katie, or are you ready for rhubarb crumble?"

Katie put down her knife and fork and sighed. "Oh, I'd forgotten what real cooking is! But I'd better not have any more. It's a long walk up that infirmary drive from the bus stop."

"Now, don't you worry yourself about that," Gary's mother assured her. "We'll leave the washing up to them –" she nodded at the two men – "and I'll drive you up there."

For a moment Katie was appalled. She didn't want Mrs Ledbetter to come with her; she wanted to see her dad on her own.

As if reading her thoughts, Mrs Ledbetter went on, "I've got a bit of shopping to do down in Armthwaite, so I'll drop you off at the infirmary and collect you any time you want."

"Oh, there's no need to collect me," said Katie. "I'll get the bus straight home."

She felt Gary and his mother exchange glances. Gary seemed about to speak, but gave up as his mother took over.

"You're more than welcome to stay here for the weekend, Katie. Your house'll be cold and cheerless, I shouldn't wonder." She looked round with satisfaction at her own high-tech, highly-polished little kitchen/diner.

But Katie was determined. "Oh, no – thanks – I need to sort some things out to take back anyway," she said. "And it'll soon warm up when I light a fire."

"But your bed'll not be aired!" protested Mrs Ledbetter.

"I'll put a bottle in as soon as I get back," Kate promised. "Really – I've got to go back home."

Mrs Ledbetter looked hard at Gary, then at her husband, but neither spoke. Suddenly, Katie realized a huge question mark hung in the air. When Gary came round to see her that evening she'd be alone in the empty house. To her annoyance, Katie blushed. "I'll be all right on my own," she assured Gary's mother. "And I've got a ton of work to do," she added.

"Not tonight, though," Gary said. "I told the gang you were coming home – we're all meeting up at Woody's."

Although she had no desire to meet the gang at the local pub disco, Katie felt she'd done enough defying for one dinner-time. "Well, I suppose I'll have a bit of time tomorrow morning," she said. "I've got to get on with an assignment."

"On your first weekend home?" said Gary's mother, pointedly. "That's a bit much, isn't it?"

"It's my fault for letting it pile up," Katie explained.

"Too busy gadding with all them young doctors, are you?" Mr Ledbetter teased.

Katie flushed and looked at the kitchen clock. "Can I just pop upstairs before we go?" she asked. And without waiting for permission, she rushed off to the bathroom.

Walking along the corridors of a strange hospital, Katie reflected how different it felt from St Ag's. And how very different she felt, being a visitor, not a nurse. Still, it was a relief to be on her own again, after the suffocating atmosphere at the Ledbetters'. Ever since Katie's mother had died, Mrs Ledbetter had tried to take over the Hardings' lives, just as she had long ago taken over the lives of her husband and her son.

She'll never have a chance with my dad, Katie smiled to herself. Nobody could take him over.

She was still smiling when she approached his bed.

"Eeh bah gum, if it isn't that Nurse 'arding," he greeted her, in a mock Yorkshire accent. "Killed any good patients lately?"

Katie laughed aloud and bent to kiss her father. "I'll kill you if you do this on me again," she chided. But she couldn't stop herself grinning at him. "Why didn't you let me know you were ill?"

"Ill? Who's ill?" He looked at her, opening his light blue eyes wide. "I just popped into the surgery for a blood-pressure check and next thing I know – here I am!"

"Well, they wouldn't have you in here unless it was necessary."

"You're right," he nodded. "They've got plenty on without me. I keep watching them slaving away and thinking about you. Are you working hard?" He looked at her closely.

"I told you, I only have one ward day; the rest is lectures and seminars."

"And a lot of homework?"

Katie nodded. "Plenty of that," she said, though she didn't tell him she should have been doing hers right then. "Now, let's have a look at your notes and see what they're doing to you." And before he could ask her any more about college work, she picked up the notes from the end of his bed and bent to read them. "Taking a lot of blood tests, aren't they?" she asked.

"They are that," he agreed. "Every blooming day they're at me. I think the lass from the lab fancies me, you know!"

Katie laughed with him and they went on to talk about his health and her life at college. Before they noticed, tea was brought round – for the patients but not the visitors.

"It's all these staff cuts," Dad explained. "You have to get one from the machine out in the corridor. Here – here's some change."

She wasn't bothered about tea, but she did feel the need for a break. It was harder work being a visitor than being on ward duty, she reflected, as she passed a group of chatting nurses at the desk. She'd often watched the visitors at St Ag's, sitting by the bed, turning away from the patient to watch the television in the corner, or glancing surreptitiously at their watches, having said all they could find to say in two minutes flat.

Well, she and her dad weren't like that, anyway; they had plenty to talk about – not least about how he was going to manage when he finally got back home. She took a polystyrene beaker of scalding tea, wrapped her hanky round it and walked back up to the ward.

Her father sat, propped by his pillows, dozing. Obviously he, too, needed a break. She stood at the end of the bed and studied his face, pale and rather dropped, now that he wasn't speaking. He looked smaller now, older, and rather worn. Tears flooded Katie's eyes; she wiped them on the back of her hand and sniffed, loudly.

"Is that you, our Katie?" Dad woke up and beamed with pleasure. "Have you got your tea, luv?"

"I have that, our Dad," she said, broadly. And they laughed together again. Katie sat down and told him about the Kelham Six and their plans for the centenary cabaret.

"I shall have to get well enough to come and see you in that," he said. "I've never missed one of your shows yet, lass."

"But you won't see me," Katie told him. "I'm producing this time."

"Must be a lot of hard work," he observed.

"Oh, you can't imagine…" Katie went on to tell him about the committee, the auditions, meetings, rehearsals, and her sketch writing.

"Seems to me you've got plenty on without training to be a nurse," he said, craftily.

"Oh, don't you worry, I do the show in my spare time," she assured him, crossing her fingers. "Keeps me out of mischief, as Mum would have said."

There was a pause, as always, when she mentioned her mother. Dad never would talk about her, never seemed to come to terms with her death even though it was more than three years ago now.

"And talking of mischief," he said, heavily humorous, "aren't you going out with Gary tonight?"

Katie's smile faded. "I suppose so," she said. "He's arranged for us to meet up with some of the old gang, you know."

"You don't sound thrilled."

She sighed. "I'm not. I just don't feel as though I belong with them any more."

"Or with Gary?" he asked her, bluntly.

She couldn't lie to him; never could. "We've been together so long, Dad, it's time to move on."

"To somebody new?"

She blushed. "There is nobody new – only a lot of new friends, colleagues, acquaintances…" Her voice trailed off miserably.

"And you're going to tell the lad, tonight, are you?" her dad prompted.

"I suppose I ought to," Katie said. "But he's working so hard for his A-levels – I don't want to upset him."

"You'll upset him a lot more if you're not honest with him."

"I knew you'd say that," she almost laughed. "But everyone's not as brave at facing the truth as you are."

"Oh, I'm not brave," he said. "I'm trembling inside all the time in this place."

Katie looked at him quickly. "You think it's something serious, Dad?" she asked.

He shook his head. "Nay, lass," he said. "You're more likely to know that than I am. Tell me nowt, these folk."

"Then you must make them tell you. Ask a lot of questions…"

"They're so busy, you know, on the run night and day. I don't like to trouble them."

"Dad, if patients weren't any trouble folk like me would be out of a job."

"Like the rest of us." Dad nodded. "Well, Sister Bland's all right – when she has the time to listen. I'll try to catch her tomorrow, see what she says."

"You could make a list of questions. We can do it together, now, if you like," she offered.

He hesitated. "Thanks, Katie, love, but I need to get my thoughts collected. I'll have a go later." And he sank back against his pillows.

He did look tired, Katie thought. He'd had enough – and so, frankly, had she.

"I'll have to be off, Dad. Gary's coming for me later and there's no fire on, no hot water…"

"I thought you'd be staying up at Ledbetters' place," he said.

"Well, I didn't really want to – you don't mind if I go home?"

"Mind? Don't be daft." He tried to sound hearty but his voice was quite weak. "But there'll be no milk in, no weekend shopping – and don't forget to air your bed…" He was almost asleep again.

"I won't. 'Bye, Dad – I'll see you tomorrow afternoon."

He opened his pale eyes. "See you, then, our Katie," he murmured. "Good luck with … tha knows!"

Chapter 8

It wasn't luck she needed so much as courage, Katie reflected as she dragged a comb through her tangled hair. And a hairdryer, she realized; this lot would certainly not dry in time for going out. In fact, just as she tugged her damp curls into shape, Gary knocked at the door.

"Coming!" she called. She gave a final, hopeful scrunch to her hair, grabbed her coat and bag and rushed downstairs. Best be ready, leave all the intimate chat till later.

"Hi – come in – just want to check the fire..." She led the way into the main room of the house.

"How was he, then?" Trust Gary to ask; he really was a nice, thoughtful lad. Katie suddenly felt rather tearful. She bent over to fix the fire guard and to hide her face. "Oh, not exactly ill," she said. "Soon got tired, though."

"Is that significant?"

She stood up straight and for the first time that day, she looked up into his eyes.

"Well, it's not like him, is it?"

Gary shook his head. "No," he agreed. "Always plenty of energy, your dad. Now, if it was mine…"

They laughed; Mr Ledbetter was well known for nodding off in odd corners, like a cat. The sound of their laughter seemed to echo in the empty house. Katie looked round hastily, as if they'd been caught out doing something wrong.

"We'd better get off, then," she said. "The bus is at twenty-past, isn't it?"

Still smiling, he nodded. "Glad you remember," he said. And before she could do it for herself, he picked up her coat and held it ready. Katie slipped her arms into the sleeves. Gary folded the coat round her, leaned over and kissed her gently below her ear.

"Been dying to do that since you got into the station," he whispered.

Katie stood, frozen, knowing that if she turned to face him he'd kiss her properly. Then the old wall clock struck the quarter and she pulled free.

"Come on!" she laughed. "We'll have to run for that bus!"

* * *

It was easy after that. The music was so loud in Woody's that she could scarcely even call a greeting to her old friends and any intimate talk was out of the question. Like everybody else, she yelled banalities, danced with various partners, sipped a couple of Cokes and tried to persuade herself that she was having a great time. Everyone else was – they missed the last bus and shared a taxi home. So the two of them weren't alone together until they stood on Katie's doorstep.

"You should have gone on in the taxi," she told him. "Melanie lives up your way."

He took the door key from her and turned the lock. "Can I come in?" he asked, quietly.

Katie nodded and led the way.

They sat on the settee by the fire, sipping rather nasty black coffee, which Katie, in her nervousness, had insisted on making, and saying nothing. It was so quiet in the little terraced house that Katie jumped when the clock gave a whirr preparatory to striking the hour.

"Midnight," she observed. "Time you were getting home." And she almost smiled at the memory of Gary, rushing out of the house at half-past eleven every Saturday night, running all the way home to get in before his mother's curfew expired.

"Time you got up to date," he said. And he put his hand into his pocket and dangled a house-key in front of her. "Mum and I have done a bit of serious talking lately."

Katie watched the key dangling like a pendulum as the clock struck twelve. "Maybe we should do a bit of serious talking," she said, when the last chime died away.

Gary put the key into his pocket and sat back. "Go ahead," he said. "I'm listening. All ears – remember?"

And, in spite of herself, Katie giggled. For she did remember the lad in their junior school who could never could get the hang of metaphors.

"…and when Miss Thomson told him to pull his socks up he bent down and tugged at them!" she said.

"And he thought he'd go blind when somebody said he was crying his eyes out," Gary joined in.

And for a moment it was as if she'd never been away. They'd shared so much of their lives, Katie reflected, it was as if they were related. Brother and sister.

That was the problem. She stopped laughing and sat up straight.

"You know what I'm going to say?" she asked him.

He nodded. "Met somebody, have you?"

"No!" she almost shouted at him. "I have not met anybody – or rather I've met lots of people but not in the sense you mean." She was angry with him, disappointed in this typical reaction.

"So you want to feel free with these new people?" he asked.

Katie sighed. "I just want to feel free, full stop," she said. "I don't want to feel you here, waiting to pass your driving test so's you can come over, waiting to pass your A-levels, waiting to join me over the Pennines. In fact," she turned now, and faced him squarely, "I don't want you to wait at all, Gary."

"You can't stop me," he pointed out. "If I choose to wait – for whatever I'm waiting for – you can't stop me."

"No, I can't," she agreed. Suddenly she felt years older. "But one of the things you're waiting for is university, isn't it? And when you get there, you'll understand how it is with me just now. You'll outgrow all this –" she gestured vaguely in the direction of the village – "and you'll want to feel free of it all."

"But you're not a part of all this now, are you?" he argued. "And if I get to university we can both be free of it." He suddenly turned to her so that the firelight shone into his eyes and she could see the pain in them. "Can't you wait, even a few months?" he asked. And his voice shook.

Katie dared not trust her own voice for a moment. Then, taking a deep breath, she said, "There's no point, Gary. By that time you'll be a different person – as I am, now."

"But our plans – me at Mulcaster, you at Brassington…"

"I'm not even sure I shall be at Brassington by then." As soon as she said it, Katie realized it was true. "I'm not as committed to nursing as I thought I'd be," she explained. "I'm doing this production and it's so creative, so important to me, I'm beginning to think I've made a mistake. Only please, don't tell Dad, will you? Or your parents either?"

Gary slowly shook his head. "You are kicking free, aren't you?" he said, quietly. "I can see why you need a bit of space… But it's all so up in the air, Katie. If we break off now, you might find you need me in a few months. Especially if your dad—"

"What's Dad got to do with this?" Katie rounded on him. "Have you heard something I haven't? Has your mother been—"

"No, no," he said hastily. "We know nothing. You know Mum – she's always surmising."

"Yes, she is," said Katie, grimly. Half of Armthwaite would have her dad dead and buried after listening to Annie Ledbetter. "But even I know rather more about medicine than she does and it's no use 'surmising', as you put it. Let's wait until the test results come before we 'surmise' anything." She stopped, unable to speak.

The remains of the fire shifted in the hearth, the room was growing cold. Katie shivered and stood up.

"I think you'd better go, Gary. I'll bet your

mother's still listening for that key in the door." She led the way into the passage. "I'm really, really sorry," she said.

Gary sighed. "I suppose I knew it was coming," he said. "But I didn't want to face it."

She heard the tears in his voice and felt her own eyes prickle. Suddenly she moved forward and hugged him, hard. "'Bye, Gary," she muttered into his jacket. "I'm so glad it was you who gave me the news about Dad."

He stood quite straight, looking over her head, not returning the hug. "I expect Mum'll be visiting him," he said. And he smiled a rather wobbly smile. "I shall miss him as much as I miss you," he said, truthfully.

"Then keep going to see him when I've gone," she urged. "Dad's very fond of you – he loves having discussions with you. Don't break up another friendship just because of me."

He nodded. "I'll see," he said, the usual Yorkshire noncommittal promise.

And he was gone.

Katie turned back into the room and built up the fire. Upstairs, she washed and cleaned her teeth swiftly then took the sleeping bag off her bed, back to the fireside. She flung herself on to the settee, wriggled into the sleeping bag, pushed her head into a cushion that reeked of her dad, and sobbed herself to sleep.

*   *   *

But she felt better the next day. Almost light-hearted. She had a breakfast of crackers and cheese, cleared out the fire and laid another, took a turn around the house with the hoover and duster, and all the time the radio played, shutting out her thoughts.

She sat on the bus to the hospital devouring a lunch of salt-'n'-vinegar crisps and making plans. She'd soon be home for Easter, so she could visit every day. If Dad was still in hospital by the end of the holiday, she'd have to come back at weekends. That would cut down rehearsal time for the cabaret, but Nick would help out. She could bring work home and study all the weekend – even write some more sketches – now there were no distractions...

Her dad's bed was neatly made up and there was no sign of him in the ward.

"Try the Day Room," suggested a bed patient. "They've all gone up there to watch the match."

The Day Room was along the corridor past Sister's office. "Sister Jane Bland – In," said the notice on the door. On an impulse, Katie looked in.

"Yes?" A surprisingly young woman turned from a computer keyboard to look at her. "Can I help you?"

"Could I have a word with you, please?" Katie asked. "About my father, Joe Harding."

The nurse smiled. "You must be Katie, his daughter – and a student nurse, I gather?" She swung her chair round. "Come on in, Katie. Your dad's watching the match on the big television set – he won't miss you for a few minutes. Coffee?"

"I'd love some," said Katie, eagerly, after a morning of milkless tea.

Katie gulped the excellent coffee, munched several digestives, and explained her problem. "So you see, if necessary, I could come home every weekend, catch up on some work and spend as much time as allowed with Dad."

"He'd be pleased about that, I'm sure, but he might even be home before that. Are there no relatives who could look after him?"

Katie shook her head. Dad's brothers were in Australia and Mum's side – well, no point in going into all that.

"Friends?" Sister was asking.

"Well, you see since the pit closed there's no Miners' Welfare so they don't meet regularly like they used to. I'll ring round a few of them, though, just to make sure they know where he is."

Sister nodded. "A young man came once or twice last week," she said, looking sharply at Katie. "Your dad seemed very fond of him."

Katie nodded. "I expect he'll come again," she said, vaguely. "And his mum as well, perhaps."

"Well, I don't think you need worry about him just now," said Sister. "It's when he gets home he'll need more help."

"When will that be?" Katie asked.

"Oh, I'm sure you know enough not to ask me that one," smiled Sister Bland. "Let's just say it won't be this week, so you can get back to your studies. We need the results of his first lot of tests and there may even be more to do."

"What do you think it is?" Katie looked directly at her.

Sister shrugged. "You know I can't answer that until the test results come in."

Katie had expected just that answer but she couldn't help feeling disappointed.

"I can tell you one thing," Sister went on. "He's very anaemic – hence the collapse – but otherwise he's a very fit person. We've given him a litre of haemoglobin this morning and he'll have one each day – it will improve his energy level."

"But how did he get so anaemic?" asked Katie.

Sister smiled. "That's what we're trying to find out, Katie. I'm sure you'll read all about it when you get back to St Ag's." She glanced up at the clock on the wall. "Meantime, I've got a few more reports to finish on this blasted machine. Whatever else you do, make sure you get some training in computers – they're the lifeline of the Health Service now."

"Oh, I did my computer course last year at college," Katie said. "That's one thing I'm quite good at."

And she suddenly remembered the row of computers in the library at St Ag's. They were used by staff for references and reports and by students for their assignments, or maybe even cabaret scripts! Faced with a keyboard and a screen, she felt sure she could produce a few sketches, a story-line, props list, running order – in fact, the whole show. Her mind already buzzing with ideas, she thanked Sister Bland and made her way down to the Day Room.

Dad, fully dressed and already looking pinker and brighter, assured her he'd be all right. He didn't want her travelling over every weekend; he'd ring her when there was news about the tests; he'd tell her when he was due to go home. Meantime she was to get back to work and not to worry.

"I'm almost enjoying myself in here," he beamed. "Bit of company, no chores, decent food – it's like being on holiday!"

"Well, you go on enjoying it, Dad," she told him. "I'll let a few of your friends know where you are – they'll be up to visit, no doubt."

"Aye, and your Gary – he'll be in as well."

Katie hesitated. "I hope he will, Dad," she said. "But he's not *my* Gary, you know."

Her dad looked at her, quizzically. "Sorted it all out, have you?"

Katie nodded and blushed. "You were right," she said. "As usual!" They laughed together and she bent to kiss him. "So make sure you get yourself right before they turn you out, and let me know how everything is – right?"

He nodded. "Right, lass. Now get on, else you'll miss that train."

As she sat in the train, Katie had time to reflect on her weekend. It had been difficult, but not impossible. Dad didn't seem to be in any kind of danger and she'd sorted things out with Gary at last. She peered out of the filthy windows, through the rain, at the rows of terraces set around the now-defunct pit-stocks. The scene was gloomy, desolate, yet she felt excited, filled with a sense of freedom, a sense of being on her own, after years of being a couple.

And tomorrow I'll make a start on that script, she promised herself.

Chapter 9

"But we're not supposed to miss lectures," Claire protested.

"I don't suppose I'll be missed at a mass lecture on ward hygiene," laughed Katie. "And with everybody in there, it's a great opportunity to get to a machine."

Claire sighed. "You might miss something important," she said. "It's our first exam in a few weeks, you know."

"I'll copy up your notes," Katie said. "And you can collect the hand-outs for me, can't you?"

So Claire agreed and Katie spent the morning in the library, apparently hard at work. It was hard work, too, but she didn't even notice time passing. It was as if the very act of working on the computer released something in her; the ideas simply poured out. A song for Claire, a medical skit on "Danny Boy", a Hospital Blues for Barbara, and a sketch between foreign doctor (Jan) and soopah-doopah Englishwoman looking for a vet for her horse – yes, the reluctant Nikki. Well, she'd not be so reluctant when she read this brilliant material!

Katie sat back and waited for the printer to push out her work. Just time to make a few photocopies, she calculated, and then a quick snack and off to … whatever it was on Monday afternoons. She was so deep into the cabaret now that she could barely focus on routine matters.

But as she left the library, clutching a folder full of treasures, routine matters suddenly focused on her!

"Ah, Katie – I've been looking for you." Sister Thomas faced her, looking grim. "Been catching up on your work?" she asked.

"Er … yes … sort of," said Katie, blushing scarlet.

"Well, I'm glad to see that," said Sister Thomas, sounding not at all glad. "If you could spare me a few minutes…?" And she swept up the corridor without waiting for an answer.

She led the way into her office, sat down behind the desk and motioned Katie to a chair in front.

"I did send a message asking you to come and see me over at Kelham some time during the weekend," she said. "But I gather you were called home urgently?"

Katie nodded, not trusting herself to speak. If she'd been summoned to Sister Thomas's flat during a weekend it must have been important. Now she remembered all Claire's warnings, all her unfiled notes, her unfinished reading ... her un-started assignment.

"And how is your father now?" Sister Thomas went on, thawing slightly.

Katie swallowed hard and explained what had happened back at home. "He's staying in hospital at least a week," she ended, "so I know he's being looked after."

"Good, that must be quite a relief," said Sister Thomas. "So you were able to get back last night?" she went on, casually.

Seeing what was coming, Katie merely nodded.

Sister Thomas's voice hardened. "Then why were you not in the lecture this morning?"

Feeling quite sick, Katie clutched at the batch of papers. "I told you," she said. "I had to catch up on some work."

"Ah, yes, your work. May I see?" She held out her hand and Katie had no alternative but to hand over the folder.

Sister Thomas read through the whole script in silence. Katie watched her closely, to see if she would smile. She didn't. Did that mean the script wasn't funny? Or was she just determined to be serious? It was suddenly very important for Katie to know.

Sister Thomas closed the folder and looked straight at Katie.

"You know, of course, that you must never miss lectures without good reason?"

"Yes, but, you see, I had all these good ideas and I wanted to get them ready for Tuesday's rehearsal and I'm going to copy up Claire's notes and—"

"And you're well behind with your project, you have not taken a single book out of the library and your ward diary was due in last Wednesday."

"I've been busy," Katie muttered.

"But not with your work," Sister Thomas pointed out.

There was silence. Katie knew Sister was right but she didn't know whether she cared about that or not. She longed to ask her what she thought of the script but even she could see that was inappropriate.

Eventually Sister spoke. "Remember your first day at Kelham?" she said. "I told you that I'd chosen your group because I could see that each one of you had something extra to give to nursing." Katie didn't reply so Sister went on. "That something must be extra to your training, Katie, not instead of it. You're here to train to be a nurse, not a theatrical producer."

Katie sighed. "I know," she said. "It's just been such hard work getting everyone together, then writing all the material…" She sighed, then looked up, a little more cheerfully. "I think I've done all that now, so I can catch up on the work quite easily, you know."

"No, I don't know, Katie. I think you underestimate the importance of studying after lectures, of keeping abreast with your notes and background reading, and keeping up with any current projects and assignments."

"I was hoping to do all that this weekend," Katie protested. "But I had to go home."

"Yes, you did," Sister Thomas agreed. "But don't you see, if your work had been up to date, missing a weekend in college would not have mattered."

Katie could not deny that, so she remained silent.

Sister Thomas, however, did not. "And then when you get back, you miss an important lecture, not to catch up on your work, but to write a script! Really, Katie, you are going to have to make up your mind just what is more important to you – nursing or amateur dramatics!"

At that moment Katie felt that she'd already made up her mind. But this was not the time to tell Sister Thomas.

"I'll catch up on this morning's notes, and my ward diary today," she promised. "And I'll do the first part of the orthopaedic assignment the rest of this week. Then I'll work every evening except Tuesday. I'll get lots of books from the library and do all my background reading at home in the holidays, while I'm looking after Dad."

"Well, that shows a better sense of priorities," agreed Sister Thomas. "And whilst you're making reparations, you'd better write a note of apology to Mr Lester-Ellis."

"What for?" Katie's heart sank. She was sure her ward-duty day was going quite smoothly now.

"It was his lecture you missed this morning. He asked for some student observations of ward hygiene in Orthopaedics – from Student Nurse Harding! Mr Lester-Ellis never forgets a name, you know…"

Katie groaned; as if she hadn't crossed Lester-Ellis enough! "I'll write it this very afternoon," she promised. Sister Thomas nodded gravely, apparently dismissing her. Katie rose, wondering whether she dare ask for her script back.

Silently, Sister Thomas offered her the folder.

"Thank you," Katie said turning to leave. At the door she paused. "What do you think of it?" she asked.

Sister Thomas looked steadily across at her. "It's very good – sharp, witty, a little naughty, but this side of good taste. I'm sure the Kelhamites will rise to it. But remember, Katie, it's not worth sacrificing your career for!"

Well, I'll decide that, thought Katie, as she slunk from the office.

Even so, she paid particular attention to the afternoon's seminar on interpersonal relationships, even going so far as to volunteer to lead a discussion after the holidays. And then she spent another two hours in the library – background reading this time – and made sure she took a stack of psychology books away with her.

It wasn't until she got back to Kelham House that she realized she hadn't seen Claire or Barbara since breakfast. Their usual lunch date had been ruined by Sister Thomas's kick in the pants. Katie grinned to herself. Of course she'd deserved it and it had been worth it just to hear someone praise her script! Whistling tunelessly, she knocked on Claire's door as she passed, but there was no reply. What a shame – she'd miss the opportunity to gloat!

As she was short of cash since paying the fare home, and as Claire wasn't around to feed her Irish treasures from her parents' hotel, Katie made a few rounds of toast and a great deal of coffee and carried on working in her room.

So she was quite relieved when someone knocked at her door.

"Come in, Claire – where on earth have you..."

But it was Nick.

"Thought I'd just check up on tomorrow's

rehearsal plans," he smiled. "Glad to see you back. News not too bad?"

"No, not from home at any rate." Katie told him very briefly about her dad then passed the folder of scripts over to him. "Thought you might like to look these over before tomorrow," she said, casually.

He sat on her bed and read them through. She tried to revise some anatomy notes but nothing went in. She heard him laugh, softly to himself, sneaked a look and saw him smile. Then suddenly he laughed aloud at something on the final page.

"Katie Harding – the Dawn French of St Ag's!" he cried. And he jumped up, pulled her to her feet and hugged her so hard she could hardly breathe. Didn't want to!

When he finally let her go, they swapped places: she flopped weakly on the bed, he sat at her desk, and re-read the script, shaking his head and smiling now and then.

"Well done that girl!" he said. "Who would have thought that rugged northern exterior hid such a brilliant funny talent?"

When he turned to smile at her, she felt weak all over again.

"Well, I'm glad you think it's worth it, anyway," she said.

"Who doesn't?" he asked.

So she told him about her interview with Sister Thomas and he laughed.

"Oh, Ann Thomas is a bit like you; she has to take her job seriously, keep us all up to the mark, but secretly she wants us to sparkle, to dazzle the establishment, especially this year. And she knows you can do that. Don't worry. Just keep the work turning over and you'll be all right." And he leaned over and patted Katie's shoulder. "I'll take a copy to work on for tomorrow's rehearsal – right?"

As he went off whistling down the corridor, Katie rubbed her shoulder thoughtfully. She'd rather imagined she'd take tomorrow's rehearsal, with all this new material; he'd taken over again! She rubbed her shoulder where he'd patted her and tried to feel angry. But she couldn't.

When she saw him in action on Tuesday evening, Katie had to admit he was just right for the job. He ran through a few of the individual pieces, timing them, offering a few suggestions, leaving the musical side very much to Theo.

Later he called everyone round him and asked Katie to present her new scripts. There was a long pause while they read them, punctuated by sniggers, giggles and, at the end, roars of laughter.

"Brilliant, Katie – it's great!"

"I don't know how you do it – I'm going to love singing this medical folk song!" Claire laughed.

"The doctor/vet sketch is so funny!" Nikki Browne told Katie. "You know, something similar happened to my great aunt Gus when she was travelling in Egypt," she smiled.

"Oh, that's great. You'll be able to bring a note of authenticity to it, won't you?"

"I?" Nikki's pale blue eyes widened. "You mean…?"

"Well, I wrote it especially for you. Even on the page it sounds like you. Come on, Nikki – you won't even have to act!"

"We'll do a read round," announced Nick. He quickly gave out parts to everyone and they read the whole script, with Theo sketching in tunes for the songs.

It was magic! Everyone worked hard, everyone enjoyed it – even, after some stuttering and stammering, Nikki Browne. At the end of the evening, Claire produced a huge tin of cookies, Barbara made coffee and they sat planning and talking until well past midnight. For the first time since she'd started on it, Katie felt that her cabaret was going to work.

"Well, I'm off – good night, everybody – learn that lot for next week's rehearsal – word-perfect, mind!" Nick waved his script at them and departed. And Katie, suddenly feeling flat, realized she had to be on the ward by seven next morning!

Chapter 10

Sister Beckwith had her important look on. Sweeping along the corridor so quickly that Katie, Jimmy and Eileen could hardly keep up with her, she led the way to one of the side rooms.

"Just pop in and make sure he's presentable," she asked Jimmy. "We'll wait for Mr Lester-Ellis and the junior doctors."

"Dr Saleem's been on duty all night," said Jimmy.

"Well, I hope she keeps awake," smiled Sister Beckwith. And it seemed to Katie that she looked straight at her. After her restless night she'd over-slept and missed breakfast in order to get to the ward on time. And now all she was doing was standing around waiting for Mr Lester-Ellis. It really didn't seem fair! Katie swallowed a yawn and peeped round Eileen's very ample back into the side room.

These rooms were kept for private patients or for the very confused elderly, who often rambled on all night and disturbed other people. And for the seriously ill – or dying. Katie was curious to see just who Mr Lester-Ellis was going to examine. Not Maudie Royston, she hoped.

But all she could see was a huge, plastered leg, held up on traction, a lot of bandages, drips and pulleys and a white mound where the sheet was supported by a cage. Somebody was in quite a mess, she thought.

"Stand up, Nurse!"

Startled by the urgency in Sister Beckwith's voice, Katie jumped to attention. Mr Lester-Ellis, Dr Karen Saleem and a couple of young housemen came bustling down the corridor.

"Good morning, Sister. Busy night, I gather." Mr Lester-Ellis nodded a greeting all round – rather vaguely, Katie was relieved to note. "Right – let's see what you've got for us..." The doctors entered the room, followed by Sister. Eileen and Katie stood at the door.

The doctors conferred, read notes, held up X-rays and otherwise ignored both staff and patient. Katie was free to peer more closely.

And wished she hadn't. The face beneath the

heavily bandaged head was grey and oddly mottled by tiny cuts and scratches, as if it had been rained on by glass. The eyes were so blackened they looked as if they'd been painted round; the shocking pink nose, huge and swollen, seemed too big for the pinched little face. Katie swallowed hard and prepared to turn away.

But in that fraction of a second the eyes opened, reddened and bloodshot, but startlingly blue and bright with intelligence. For a moment they looked at Katie as if trying to convey a message. Katie had an urge to run to the bedside, to say soothing things, hold a hand... Conscious of the curious glances around her, she merely smiled at the patient, wide and hard, and nodded, as if she understood. The bruised lids closed over the sharp blue eyes and the patient sighed, as if satisfied about something.

"Well, he's conscious." Mr Lester-Ellis glanced in Katie's direction. "You seem to have a remarkable effect on the young man," he commented.

Katie flushed and looked down at her trembling hands.

"Well, we can't do anything for a day or two," Mr Lester-Ellis went on. "Put him on the theatre list for Monday – the bruising should be down by then. I'll have a go at one of the legs at least." Mr Lester-Ellis turned to Sister. "And keep stirring him up – talk to him and so on. We must keep him conscious."

To Katie's horror he paused at the door and looked hard at her. "Student Nurse Harding, isn't it?"

Speechless, Katie just nodded.

"Right, Student Nurse Harding," he suddenly barked, "I received your note – now's your chance to redeem yourself. Keep the patient entertained and make a full report in your next ward diary – two birds with one stone, eh?" And he almost smiled as he swept on.

So that whole, long day and into the evening – well past her duty hours – Katie sat in the little room with the patient. She read the rather sparse notes: the crashed motor-bike, multiple fractures, facial lesions, trauma, shock, pillion passenger dead, police awaiting statement. Poor lad! she thought. No wonder he wanted to sleep it all off.

But it was her job to keep him conscious. All day she stroked his good arm, tapped his hand, gave him sips of water through the feeder, asked him questions, and talked, talked, talked, about anything, everything.

"Can you remember your name?" She knew it already, of course, but it was important that he knew it too.

"Philip," he murmured.

"Philip who?"

"Philip … Phil…" He drifted off again.

"Come on, Philip," she urged him, brightly. "Tell us your surname…"

"…your address…"

"…your telephone number…"

"…your parents' address…"

"…your girlfriend's…" No, she decided, remembering the dead pillion passenger, scrap that one.

"…your kind of music…"

"…your favourite group…"

"…your football team…"

"…what you like to eat…"

"…what you drink…"

"…where you've been for holidays…"

And so on, over and over and over all day.

Occasionally, Sister Beckwith would come in, check the drips and nod approvingly. She insisted that Katie took a break in her office at lunch-time – ordered coffee and a sandwich from the canteen – and Jimmy brought her cups of tea at regular intervals, but otherwise she was left alone with Philip.

By early evening his eyes were open more than closed and he was refusing to answer her questions.

"I've just told you that," he said.

"Just checking," Katie smiled. Well, at least he was remembering her questions and answering sensibly – all good indications of consciousness returning.

Then, "Where's Jackie?" he asked suddenly.

Katie's heart sank. "Who?" She played for time.

"Jackie ... was with me..."

"Jackie's not here, Philip. Sister will know more than I do. I'm only a student, you know, they tell us nothing."

She'd chickened out, she knew, but it wasn't her job to break the news to him. For once, she was glad she was only a lowly student.

At seven o'clock she was hoarse and exhausted and Night Sister insisted that she go back to Kelham. Philip was dozing and there was little danger of his relapsing into unconsciousness now.

"Good night, Philip. Sleep well," she whispered, squeezing his good hand.

"...in the morning," he murmured.

"Yes, see you, then," Katie hedged.

She passed Sister on the corridor, leading a couple of policemen into the ward, obviously going to take a statement from Philip. For a moment Katie wanted to rush up and warn them not to disturb "her" patient but then she shrugged, smiled at herself and went on her way. She was off duty now, and Philip, no longer "her" patient, was in the competent hands of Sister.

Passing through the unfamiliar, evening-time wards, filled with visitors, she suddenly remembered that other hospital; she hadn't rung Dad yet. She hadn't caught up on her studying, either. And she'd missed a lunch-time meeting with Barbara, Nick and Tina Brookes about the budget for the show – but that didn't seem to matter. It was as if she'd been enclosed in another world for a long, long time. She felt the familiar mixture of exhaustion and excitement like she had after rehearsals. But underneath this tiredness now was a feeling of satisfaction, deeper, more lasting than the usual "high".

The news from Armthwaite was good. Dad came to the phone and chatted happily about his high blood-count and his healing stomach ulcer, which had caused internal bleeding and the anaemia.

"I'll be going home in a few days," he told her, happily. "But don't you go interrupting your work, Katie, lass, not till the holidays. I've got Mrs Eckington coming in every day – she's a home-help now, you know, and Ted Gibb's been to see me – we're in the middle of a great chess battle, so he's going to share my meals-on-wheels, and then there's Gary..."

"He's still visiting, then?" she asked, pleased that Gary had taken her advice.

"Oh, aye. Seems to like to get out of that house, you know, what with swotting for his exams and all. Brought a lass with him yesterday – Melody, was it?"

"Melanie – Melanie Tapps, was it?" And Katie was surprised by a sudden pang of resentment.

"Aye, that's the lass. Nice little thing she is – bit young, I thought."

"She is – barely sixteen I should think."

"Aye well, p'raps he's had enough of older women," Dad teased.

Katie chose to ignore that.

But he was right; she did feel a lot older than the gang at home – especially tonight.

At Kelham there was more good news.

"Full-time nursing already?" Barbara grinned, when Katie staggered into the kitchen, and heated up more soup.

"You get that down you, gal," she ordered, plonking the now familiar blue bowl down in front of Katie. "I'll go call Nick."

Katie sipped the pungent broth blankly; she was so tired she leaned over her bowl, half dozing, steaming her face as if she was in a hot bath.

Then Barbara came back with Nick Bone.

"Well, Katie – glowing with pride and success?" he said.

Wishing she wasn't glowing at all, Katie sat up straight and wiped her steamy face. "What do you mean?" she asked.

"Well, in the first place, I hear you've been mopping a fevered brow and saving a lad's life…"

Katie really did blush this time. "Rubbish," she protested. "I only kept him awake. So what's in the second place?" she asked hurriedly.

"Well, whilst you were unavoidably detained

saving a life or two, Barbara did the best PR job I've ever witnessed." Nick came over and sat beside Katie. "Tina Brookes has given us a great vote of confidence and a great deal of money." He beamed at her and clapped his arms around her shoulders. "The Kelham Kit-Kat Cabaret will be the mid-week event of the Centenary celebrations. Congratulations, Katie!"

Not trusting herself to turn to Nick, not when his face was so close to hers, Katie looked in amazement at Barbara.

"Yeah – well done, Katie – I couldn't have persuaded Tina unless I had a really good show to offer her." Barbara came over and sat at the table.

Katie looked, dazed, from one to the other. It was all too much. She'd spent the day persuading herself that she was made for nursing and now they were telling her she was a successful producer!

"Thanks to you two as much as to me," she murmured. "I couldn't handle the financial side – and you've done all the directing so far, Nick…"

Nick squeezed her shoulder. "The important thing is that we're well on our way to success. Now we know the budget, we can give Nikki the go-ahead for sets and costumes…"

"Nikki? But she said there was nothing she could do…"

"Typical upper-class understatement." Barbara dismissed Nikki's modesty. "She may not be able to act, sing or dance, but she's got some very useful contacts. Some second cousin of hers is in the theatre – he can do us a great deal on costume hire. Her aunt's in advertising in a big way – her firm's going to do posters and programmes. And, what's more, Little Miss Modesty herself can wield a mean paintbrush – she's going to do all the sets! Everything's under control, Katie. All we need now is someone to pull it all together!"

Nick leaned his head on his hand and grinned straight at her.

Katie's bones turned to jelly. Suddenly she felt drained. "It'll be a load of work," she protested feebly. "I can't..."

"Oh, yes, you can!" He leaned forward and she felt the sharp, blue gaze of his eyes on hers. "You can't stop now – it's all running. You're going to be quite a celebrity at St Ag's, Katie Harding!"

Chapter 11

Being a "celebrity" was hard work. Katie had scarcely time enough to draw breath: evenings and weekends filled with rehearsals, working days with lectures, seminars, notes and textbooks. Luckily the exams were not until after the Easter break; Katie promised herself a solid week's revision at home.

Meantime, the Centenary Committee was now meeting every week. Not that Katie minded that – she always managed to find a place next to Nick nowadays and that made even the reports of the finance committee worth sitting through!

She was dismayed, however, when Mr Lester-Ellis spoke of his grave reservations about the parade and the Open Day.

"I must remind the committee that security will be a great problem," he glowered. "In view of the incidents we've all read and heard of, where interpolators have insinuated themselves into hospitals, I strongly recommend we abandon the idea of an Open Day."

Groans all round.

"But it's been on the publicity for months!" Tina Brookes protested. "We can't just withdraw it now."

"If I might make a suggestion." Nick held up his hand. Lester-Ellis nodded slightly. "We already have the police involved with traffic control – I'm sure if someone as influential as Mr Lester-Ellis had a word with the Chief Constable he could arrange for a few plain-clothes people to be posted around St Ag's..."

Mr Lester-Ellis, thoroughly softened up, had to agree, and before he could think up any further objections Tina Brookes flashed him a smile and stood up.

"We're proposing to offer all committee members one free ticket to the Centenary Ball," she said. "It's a mere token of our thanks for all the time you've put in. I'd have liked to have made it a double ticket, but I'm afraid your partners will have to pay full price, like anyone else."

"Well, it's a gesture, anyway," Nick murmured in Katie's ear. "And we've certainly earned it, haven't we?"

Katie nodded, not daring to look up from her agenda sheet. She and Nick would get a ticket each, so they could go to the Ball together without paying anything. On the other hand, it might be a generous gesture on their part to share half the cost with a partner. Was that what he would do? Well, for once in her impetuous life, she'd play the waiting game – "sit still and say nowt," as Dad would say.

But it didn't work: Nick never mentioned the Ball again, even when they were alone together, drawing up the rehearsal schedule for next term.

"You see, we'll have only a week or two clear," Katie told him. "There's exam week – nobody will want to rehearse then…"

"They might – as a relaxation," he said. "We'll get Theo to offer solo rehearsal sessions. And we can get on with building the sets…"

Katie groaned. "There's the furniture for the actual club, the costumes, and the Kabaret set… How will we ever fit it all in?"

"Oh, Katie, over-conscientious as ever." He patted her hand. "Now, just get off home and look after your dad – and your revision. And don't even think about the centenary for a whole week. I won't, I assure you."

"Are you going home?" she asked. She'd always wondered about his private – very private – life.

"Oh, I'm off to do a bit of visiting, that's all," he said, evasive as ever. And he smiled, that easy, open smile which had so irritated her once. Now, it charmed her. If only he would mention the ticket for the Ball!

Once home, Katie found it surprisingly easy to forget her worries. To her delight, Dad was in great form. He was feeling much better, back within the circle of his old friends and ex-workmates, playing darts and dominoes and taking gentle walks along the lanes – often to the pub where they all met.

With Mrs Eckington cleaning the house, and the meals-on-wheels delivering Dad's dinner, Katie had no excuse to give up her revision plans. By the end of the week, she felt as if she'd re-lived every lecture she'd ever heard.

"Well, lass, I hope it's not been too boring for you back home with your old dad," her father teased, on her last evening.

"It's been very useful – and anyway, I don't seem to have seen very much of my old dad!" she replied.

"Not seen much of anybody, have you?" He looked at her knowingly.

"No – but that was part of my plan." She was quiet for a moment, thinking how different this holiday would have been with Gary in tow. Revising together, long walks up the moors... She sighed.

"You did the right thing by Gary, you know," Dad said, reading her thoughts.

"Well, at least I can go back to college well-prepared for the exams," she smiled ruefully.

"And ready to work on the show, I'll bet."

"You will come and see it, won't you?"

"I will that," he assured her. "Ted's going to drive me over. He can't wait to meet up with your cabaret girls!"

"I'll warn them," she grinned. "Oh, it's been great to see you well again, Dad."

"It's been great to see you so happy, Katie, lass," he said. "And to see you working so well. I did wonder – last time – whether this show business wasn't getting in the way of your real work."

Katie grinned, remembering Claire's words. "Well, it did at one time," she admitted honestly. "But I've got it all worked out now."

And it seemed she had. The week's revision meant that the exams went quite smoothly for Katie. She had enough time and energy to keep a check on the music rehearsals as well as the progress of the set and costumes. Suddenly it all seemed to be falling into place.

Even Sister Thomas was her usual smiling self.

"I've put you into Ophthalmics for your next placement, Katie," she said at the Tuesday tutorial. "I know you've a lot on with the show, and Wednesday is Ophthalmics out-patients clinic. A good experience for you but not so demanding as the wards."

"Oh, thank you, Sister," said Katie. "The Kelham Six won't let you down – I promise!"

"I'm sure they won't, Katie – not with you driving them on," laughed Sister Thomas.

But it didn't feel like driving now, Katie reflected. All her performers seemed to know what they were doing and most of them were doing very well by now, thanks to their talent – and her direction, she grinned to herself.

"*Everything's coming up roses…*" She warbled her way along the corridor to get herself a coffee. She burst happily through the kitchen door, then stopped.

Two faces, bent close together over some sheets of paper on the kitchen table, looked up, startled. Barbara and Nick were going through the costings.

Katie looked back at them as they sat, knee to knee at the kitchen table, dark head close to fair mop. Nick always had this knack of intimacy, she reflected. And she wondered if he practised it on herself – or on many other women. He said something soft and low into Barbara's ear and she giggled softly, put out a hand to touch his shoulder. Katie felt all her previous ebullience fade; she looked away.

"Coffee anyone?" she asked very cheerfully.

"No thanks – we've just had one," said Barbara, answering for both of them.

Both of them! Katie leaned on the worktop and

waited for the kettle to boil, feeling suddenly gloomy. The others went on with their work, checking and double-checking, talking soft and low. It was obvious they were far too engrossed in their work – or something – to chat.

Katie made her coffee and was wondering how to make her getaway without showing the irritation she so strongly felt, when Jan called in to ask her to come down to the basement to hear his new jazz violin arrangement. Relieved, she followed him downstairs and settled to another hour's rehearsal. When she returned from the basement, both Barbara and Nick had gone.

Both of them together? she wondered.

Chapter 12

Katie sped down to the basement of St Ag's to check on the progress of the cabaret set. Would anything ever be done on time? she asked herself. One week to go and the Community Centre still looked more like a church youth club than a sleazy nightclub.

"How are we going to get this lot upstairs?" she asked Nikki Browne, who was using her lunch hour to paint the set.

"Have a word with the porters, will you? I couldn't possibly," said Nikki.

Katie groaned: it seemed to her that all she ever did these days was "have a word" with people – the caretakers complaining about the mess in the basement, the Catering Manager refusing to loan the furniture, the amateur electrician who'd blown the fuses on the lighting board, the panicking actors, the coughing singers, the absentee musicians... Sometimes it felt as if she was running the whole hospital, not just a one-night show!

But at least the stage was going to look good; Nikki Browne's talent had surprised everybody – including, Katie surmised, herself.

"Oh, anyone could slap a bit of paint here and there..." she told Katie now.

"When I slap paint it's never here – it's mostly well over there!" laughed Katie. "Face it, Nikki, in this department you're well ahead of any of us. On the other hand," she added. "I might just be able to persuade a team of porters to shift this lot upstairs. See you! Don't forget your run-through this evening!"

"How could I forget?" Nikki groaned. "I'm filled with terror every time I think about that horse sketch."

"Don't worry – you'll be great – the image of your great aunt Gus!" Katie left Nikki wondering whether that was a compliment or an insult and dashed off to "have a word" with the head porter.

If they could shift the set on Friday, the Kelhamites could erect it on Saturday ready for the dress rehearsal on Sunday, she planned. Well, it was all coming together at last!

*　　*　　*

Centenary Week started on a chill, grey Sunday morning with a hint of rain in the air.

"Not a good day for a procession!" Katie observed as she walked with Claire up to the cathedral for the thanksgiving service.

"They'll maybe call it off if the rain sets in," suggested Claire.

"Well, a bit of rain never hurt anybody," Katie said, quoting her dad. "Still, I'm glad we're not marching in the parade. I don't want to lose any of my cast!"

"What on earth do you mean?" Claire asked sharply.

"They might catch cold," said Katie. "You'll catch one yourself if we don't get a move on!" She tugged at Claire's cloak and they scuttled through the drizzle together.

In the dim light of the cathedral, Katie sat with her eyes closed, though more for relaxation than prayer. She felt a little awkward with Claire, on her knees, at the side of her. And surprised – was Claire a Catholic? And if she was, should she be here in a Protestant church?

Before Katie could ask, the organist embarked on the processional anthem, the two girls stood up together and Centenary Week had begun!

A feeble shaft of sunshine broke through the clouds as they emerged from the cathedral, and the air felt milder. Katie had a glimpse of Nick Bone's fair head moving amongst the crowd – accompanied by someone wearing a very striking hat above well-padded shoulders – Tina Brookes, no doubt. Katie felt the sun disappear, leaving the morning chill and damp once more.

"Do you really want to wait for the procession?" she asked Claire.

Claire shook her head. "I think I'll get back to Kelham's," she said. "I did promise to help Nikki with the final touches to the stage curtains."

Katie dragged her eyes away from Tina and Nick. It certainly didn't look as if Nick Bone was going to be much help with the final touches to anything.

"I'll come with you," she said. "There's still a lot to be done before this afternoon."

The dress rehearsal went ominously smoothly. Everyone in the right place at the right time, singers, musicians, jugglers, dancers and comics all well-drilled, word-perfect. The smattering of audience laughed knowingly at the hospital sketches and were almost in hysterics at Nikki Browne's hauteur when she mistook her husband's doctor for her horse's vet. And even Katie had to admit that Nick's smooth patter and excellent timing held the show together.

"Well, then, that's it," Katie observed to Jan as they sorted music sheets at the interval.

"That's it – a hit!" said Jan, smiling proudly at his joke.

"Well, I don't know about that." Katie frowned. "You know what they say about dress rehearsals."

"What do they?" asked Jan.

Katie groaned. "Bad dress rehearsal – good first night," she repeated, parrot-fashion.

"But we have only a first night – no others," said Jan. "We must be good then also."

"You will be, Jan," Katie assured him. "The only problems now are purely logistical." She gazed round the cheerless hall.

"Excuse me – logis… What it is?"

"Logistics," Katie explained. "Like, how can we transform this place into a glamorous nightclub in just two days!"

"Well, if anyone can do log-is-tics – you can," said Jan. "And is there not another saying about the theatre? Something about being all right on the night?"

And Katie couldn't help smiling at him. "Yes," she said. "Let's hope it will be!"

On Wednesday evening Katie stood in front of the curtain and surveyed her little empire. You really wouldn't know it was the same place, she thought. The pink-shaded lamps, small round tables and bentwood chairs had come from a failed restaurant that Nikki Browne "just happened to know". Katie smiled to herself; whatever else this show did, it had certainly brought Nikki out of her shell.

Nikki's shimmering curtain shifted and the nightclub girls came mincing down to the tables, wearing shiny black lycra tops, tiny scarlet skirts and opaque black tights.

"How do we look, Katie?" one of them asked. She stuck a long, black leg in front and parted her shiny red lips in an inane grin.

"Wonderful! Just keep up the characters I showed you," Katie told them. "No keen nursing students tonight – froth and flirt and get some good drinks sales – right?"

"Right!" they assured her. They picked up their little trays and stood ready to greet their "customers". The Kelham Kabaret Klub was ready to open!

Katie took a last look at the scene then made her way backstage. Someone was already busy in the dim light of the wings; she went forward to see if she could help – and stopped. A close-cropped, dark head pressed against a blond mop of curls, whispering low, laughing intimately. Barbara and Nick Bone.

Katie quickly turned away to the musicians' corner, where she made some pretence of checking the running order again.

"Everything all right, Katie?" Nick was at her side, now, smiling and relaxed in spite of the responsibility for running the whole show. "Come to wish me luck, have you?"

"Actually, it's bad luck to say that," she told him, coldly. "You should say 'break a leg!'"

He laughed, his easy, confident laugh. "Well, this is as good a place as any to do that," he said. "But it would be a shame to ruin the show!"

"It's to ward off bad luck – like crossing your fingers," said Katie. "So – break a leg!" She moved to get past him.

But he took hold of her shoulders and swung her round to face him. "It's a great show, Katie – we'll try not to let you down." And he hugged her, hard. For a moment they stood, pressed close in the dimness. Then, "Mustn't smudge my make-up," he laughed. "We'll have to wait till later!"

But later, after the show, Katie was otherwise engaged.

"Well done – I'm that proud of you!" Her father's few words meant more to Katie than all the hearty – and hasty – congratulations backstage. The cast and musicians were rushing to change, ready for the disco, taking very little notice of their producer, Katie felt. They'd seemed almost relieved when she announced she had to go and talk to her dad.

"Well, I'm glad to see you." She hugged him. "Now, where's Ted?" She looked past her father to greet the friend who had driven him over the Pennines. But Ted wasn't there.

Gary was. "Hello, Katie!" he said. "Told you I'd

be over as soon as I passed my test!"

"Congratulations!" Katie swallowed hard and tried to look cool. "Thanks for bringing Dad over to the show."

"My pleasure!" He looked at her and smiled, friendly, not at all intimate.

Well, that was what she'd wanted, wasn't it?

"Er … we ought to have a coffee and a bit o' something before that drive back, Gary, lad…" Dad looked hopefully at Katie and she knew he was expecting her to stay with them.

Even as they stood there, rather awkwardly waiting for her to take the lead, Theo announced the first dance at the Kelham Kabaret Klub. Katie remembered Nick's taste for "real" dancing and his promise to see her after the show. She looked from her father's proud face to Gary's eager smile and dismissed all thoughts of Nick Bone.

"We'll get a coffee in the staff café," she said, brightly. "This way." She led them out of the murky Kabaret Klub into the harsh lights of the real world. One coffee and she'd excuse herself, she thought, feeling rather mean.

But Gary wasn't in a hurry. He sat over his coffee and scones, telling Katie all his news just as if they'd never parted.

"…and after the exams, I've got a part-time job up at the labs – you know, where I did my work-experience last year? Well, I might even stay with them and take their training course," he told her. "I've gone off the university idea…"

"You mean you want to stay in Armthwaite?" Katie asked, incredulous, then embarrassed at her dismissal of her home town.

"Well, you have to take a job when it's there," said Gary, sounding as if he was quoting somebody – his mother probably. "They have a sponsor scheme – I could do my degree later while I'm still earning…"

He sounded older, Katie thought, with all this talk of money and jobs. And he was already making a new life without her – quite happily, it seemed. Happier than she was?

" 'Course, you'll be nearer Melody," Dad seemed to prompt him.

Gary flushed. "You remember Melanie Tapps?" he asked Katie.

"Oh, yes, I remember her," she said. "She lives near you, doesn't she?"

Gary nodded and quickly looked down at his plate. But he was smiling, Katie noticed, and for a moment she half-envied Melanie. She'd have no problems finding someone to take her to a dance. She yawned suddenly, then stifled it.

"Sorry," she said. "It's been quite a week!"

Mr Harding consulted his watch and then stood up. "Aye, we'd better be off, then. Soon be your summer holiday, Katie – we'll be seeing you then, eh?"

As they walked along to the car park, Katie suddenly felt rather depressed. The thought of the summer break in Armthwaite was not very tempting. And even back here at St Ag's there was nothing to look forward to. Her show was now over; her own big moment – and all she'd done to celebrate was have a coffee with Dad and her happily-ex-boyfriend! She stood in the visitors' car park waving Gary and Dad on their way and feeling like the last person in the world. And she still had no partner to take her to the Centenary Ball!

She walked across to Kelham's as if through treacle. The flow of adrenalin she usually got after a show seemed to have passed her by; all she wanted to do now was to crawl into bed and crash out, preferably for the next few days!

Kelham's was utterly quiet; obviously everyone else was still whooping it up over at the Community Centre Kabaret Klub. Well, let them; she couldn't face that place now. Tomorrow they'd be stripping the set, the furniture, packing the costumes away and it would be all over. Katie stood in the dimly-lit hall, fumbling for the key to her room, which seemed to be hiding at the bottom of her bag. What was the matter with the lights? She looked around the walls for the main switches.

Suddenly she felt herself lifted off the ground! "Aaahhh!" she screamed. But somebody rushed her across the hall and straight through the common room doorway. Then she felt herself lowered on to a low table where she stood, blinking in the bright light, trying to make sense of what was going on.

"Ladees and gennlemen!" Her "porter", Nick Bone, gave a flourishing bow. "May I present to you, that genius of Kelham House, that gift to the nursing profession, that…"

"Oh, shut up, Nick!" Katie struggled furiously to get off the table, but found herself held firmly round the waist.

"…Ms Katie Harding – director, producer, and student nurse!" Nick finished. "A toast – to Katie!"

And Katie, her eyes now used to the light, looked round and saw that the common room was crowded with people – most of them *her* people. Cast, musicians, waiters, hostesses – they were all there, glasses raised.

"Katie! To Katie!" they said.

And Katie Harding found herself in tears.

"Speech! Speech!" they called.

"Oh – I can't – I haven't got anything to say – yes, I have!" Katie stopped and took a deep breath. "Where's my drink, then?" she demanded.

"I don't think that's quite what we meant by a speech, dahling," said Barbara, handing up a glass of something fizzy.

But Katie held her glass up to the light. "To The Six!" she said. "Les Six, Theo tells me, were brilliant, rather quirky composers in France – well, thank you, Our Six, for your quirky, brilliant talents and for all your support. I couldn't have done any of it without you. Cheers! Ow! Aaatchoo!" She took a sip at the glass and a fizz of bubbles into her nose. "It's not lemonade, then," she laughed as Nick helped her down.

And suddenly – it wasn't just the champagne – her energy was flowing again. She chatted and laughed with everyone. Sister Thomas was there, pink with the wine and the pride in her own special students, in earnest conversation with Tina Brookes. And there were Theo and Jan – with Claire looking lovelier and happier than she'd looked for weeks, and Nikki Browne with a rather dishy chap in a tuxedo. And some of the day students too! No wonder everyone had been so preoccupied after the show; they were off to get the party ready for her!

Suddenly it occurred to her that Dad and Gary might have been in on the plot. That would account for her father's sudden need for coffee – and for Gary's chatting on and on about his plans.

"Oh, yes, I arranged that with your father at the interval," smiled Sister Thomas. "We needed a little time to get things ready over here. I felt we Kelhamites deserved our own little celebration tonight. You've done so much hard work in this room since you arrived, it was time to use it for fun." She looked over Katie's shoulder and seemed to nod at someone.

It was Tina Brookes, carrying a huge bouquet.

"For you, Katie, with thanks from the Centenary Committee for all your hard work. We've all agreed that this was the most brilliant entertainment the first-year students have ever produced."

Blushing, trembling, Katie took the bouquet and thanked Tina. She was followed by Jan, who handed her a large white envelope.

"From the cast and musicians – all of us who took part in your show. We thank you, Katie, for all the hard work – and all the fun!"

It was a very generous book token with a card signed by everyone in the cast.

"Thank you – thanks, everybody! I promise not to spend it on medical books..." Katie smiled all round. Then Theo struck up a chord, and people moved off to dance.

"Do you forgive your kidnapper enough to dance with him?" Nick came smiling over to her.

Katie hesitated. This man seemed to think he could charm any woman he wanted. Well, she wasn't going to join his fan-club – was she?

She sighed. "I think I'd better get this lot out of the way," she indicated her flowers. "And I'm awfully tired..."

Nick raised his eyebrows. "Pity," he said. "I thought we might get in a bit of practice before Saturday."

Her heart lurched. She looked at him, startled. "Saturday?" she said.

"Saturday – the Grand Centenary Ball – for which we each have a ticket. I know you've had far more important things to think about so I didn't want to bother you – but can I have an answer now, please, Katie?"

"Depends on the question," she smiled.

He moved closer, speaking softly, seriously, without a trace of the charming smile. "May I take you to the Centenary Ball, Katie Harding?"

Katie suddenly remembered the first day she'd seen him in that room. He'd been silent then, detached, gloomy, even. Maybe there was more to Nick Bone than easy charm? She looked up into his eyes – was that expression really anxious?

"Thought you'd never ask," she grinned. "Shall we dance?"

Chapter 13

"And so Cinderkatie is going to the Ball – and with Prince Charming himself!" Claire teased Katie next morning.

Katie had the grace to blush. "So what's wrong with a bit of charm?" she demanded. "I thought the Irish were famous for it."

"Of course!" Claire gave a little bow. "It's called blarney, you may recollect."

"Oh, I think Nick's got more to him than that," said Katie.

"He must have if you're so ready to defend him. Anyway, I'm just pleased that we've all got tickets. At one time I didn't think Jan would let me pay for his."

"But you used your Irish charm on him?" Katie laughed.

Claire blushed. "Well, Jan's not easily charmed, you know," she said. With a touch of regret, Katie noted.

They were back in routine now – off to lectures, rushing on with assignments, catching up with ward notes. It felt to Katie as though the Centenary celebrations were over – in spite of the prospect of the Ball on Saturday. Claire was right about being lucky to get tickets – they were harder to come by than Cup Final seats now.

So the Kelham Kabaret Klub was dismantled, the costumes packed away and Katie went back to being a mere student nurse again. But she didn't mind at all, now. The show had been a great challenge, and it had been fun. But now she had to get on with the rest of her life – in nursing, of that she was certain.

In the more immediate future, though, she had a problem. What on earth could she wear to the Ball? Katie had never been to anything more formal than an Armthwaite College disco; she didn't possess a ball-gown. And she certainly couldn't buy one.

"Just wear a little black number," Barbara advised. "You don't have to look like a bridesmaid these days."

But Katie's only "black number" was her best velvet trousers and she'd already worn them to the show.

"I could lend you my long cotton frock," Claire suggested. But she was five feet six and Katie barely touched five feet. And anyway, Katie wasn't the Laura Ashley type.

Dad's card arrived on Friday morning. Recognizing the handwriting, Katie didn't open it until her coffee break. It was a sepia picture of Armthwaite Mills with a laconic "Congratulations – hope it was a good party – love Dad."

And a cheque.

"Wow!" Katie breathed. "Enough for a new dress."

"Oh, Katie – I'm so glad. We'll all come with you tomorrow to choose it," said Claire.

"No, you won't," said Katie.

So it was with lots of trepidation that she dressed on Saturday night. Make-up was no bother – with her summer freckles she needed only a twist of the mascara brush and a touch of pearly lipstick to liven up her face. Her newly-cut hair was still damp; it clung in curly tendrils round her face, like a baby's. Katie pushed it into shape with her fingers, scrunching the curls on top and twisting to try to see the back in the small dressing-table mirror. She was concentrating so hard that she jumped when somebody knocked.

"Come in!" she called.

Claire drifted in wearing a sea-green chiffon gown that clung and floated at the same time, making her look like a Celtic princess. Her thick black hair was tied up in a knot, with a green ribbon trailing down.

"Do you think I look too tall?" she asked.

Katie got up to hug her. "You look marvellous," she said. "Like someone out of King Arthur's court."

Claire gimaced. "But six inches taller," she said. "Jan's barely as tall as I am."

"Nonsense. I noticed when you danced at the party after the show – he's exactly as tall as you are."

"Really?" Claire looked relieved. "Well, so long as I wear my little gold pumps…" She looked around the room. "And come on, Katie – everybody's ready except you. Let me help you into your dress."

The others were all waiting down in the hall as Claire and Katie came downstairs. Barbara in red, tight and slinky, holding Theo's arm; Nikki in softly-billowing cream silk, with a tall young man in a white dinner jacket: Jan – taller in his hired DJ – standing at the foot of the stairs looking up at Claire as if he'd like to eat her.

And Nick Bone, waiting by the open door, looking strong and stocky in his ex-navy tropicals, his blond hair gleaming close to his head for once. He turned to the stairs and his jaw dropped – devoid of charm for once – as he watched Katie coming towards him.

Her dress was very simple – even with Dad's

cheque it had to be – bronze, green and burgundy shooting through the crushed taffeta skirt with a strapless top revealing her creamy white shoulders, scattered with golden freckles. Her hair was fluffed now, in a bright reddish halo around her glowing face, echoed by her only piece of jewellery: Grandad's albert, a heavy, gold watch-chain in old-fashioned red gold.

Everyone smiled at this unusually elegant Katie as she stepped – carefully – down into the hall.

"Hi, everybody. Ready for off?" she said breezily. Then, as she saw Nick's dazed expression, she paused.

Nick swallowed hard. "Hello, Katie. You look wonderful," he said, huskily. He held out his arms.

But Katie merely took his hand. "In case I fall down again," she teased. And she knew he remembered their first meeting here in the hall – was it only months ago?

She turned to the others, "Come on, we'll take the Centenary Ball by storm," she said. "Allons Les Six – Kelhamites for ever!"

And striding out together, Katie Harding and Nick Bone led the way to St Ag's Centenary Ball.

Read about the nurses' next term at St Ag's in...

NURSES

Claire's Conquests

Claire's looking forward to getting back to St
Ag's for the new term. Working in Accident
and Emergency sounds so exciting – and of
course Jan will be back too. She can't wait to
be with him again...

But somehow the term doesn't work out quite
as she'd planned. It's tough on the ward – and
so easy to make mistakes... Jan seems cold
and distant... And then there's her dashing
cousin Patrick. He seems keen to pay her *lots*
of attention – but what *exactly* is he up to?

All the thrills of a busy Emergency Room, from the ever-popular Caroline B. Cooney.

EMERGENCY ROOM

CITY HOSPITAL. EMERGENCY ROOM. And the evening has only just begun...

6.00 p.m. Volunteers Diana and Seth arrive – eager to help save lives...

6.38 p.m. Emergency – gun shot wound – victim of a deadly drug battle...

6.55 p.m. Suspected cardiac in Bed 8. Another routine heart attack? Not for Diana...

7.16 p.m. All systems go – Alec, sixteen, clings to life by a thread.

This is the Emergency Room. Precious seconds are ticking away, and Diana and Seth hold the balance between life and death...

Dare you unlock...

THE
SECRET
DIARIES

Dear Diary...

When Joanna starts at her new school, she
suddenly has a lot to write about in her diary.
For one thing, she's fallen madly in love...

I'm not sure I want to write this down, Diary...

But then she finds her love leads her to write
about other things. Betrayal and danger.
Maybe even murder...

*At least I know my secret will be safe with you.
Though you wouldn't think safety was a big
concern of mine. Not after I got involved in such
terrible things...*

Discover Joanna's shocking secrets in
The Secret Diaries by Janice Harrell:

I Temptation
II Betrayal
III Escape

•PATSY KELLY•
INVESTIGATES

When Patsy starts work at her uncle's detective agency, her instructions are very clear. Do the filing. Answer the phone. Make the tea. *Don't* get involved in any of the cases.

But somehow Patsy can't help getting involved...

And it's not just the cases she has to worry about. There's Billy, too. Will she ever work out what she *really* feels about him...?

•PATSY KELLY•
INVESTIGATES

Anne Cassidy

Look out for:

A Family Affair
The End of the Line